THE BLUSHING HARLOT

MERRY FARMER

THE BLUSHING HARLOT

Copyright ©2019 by Merry Farmer

Cover design by Erin Dameron-Hill (the miracle-worker)

ASIN: B07PHVSRG8

Paperback ISBN: 9781090684653

Click here for a complete list of other works by Merry Farmer.

If you'd like to be the first to learn about when the next books in the series come out and more, please sign up for my newsletter here: http://eepurl.com/RQ-KX

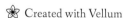 Created with Vellum

For Jess...
...who was the first one to read my schmexy books

CHAPTER 1

LONDON – AUTUMN, 1815

M iss Dobson's Finishing School purported itself to be London's premier institution for refining young women, aged eighteen to twenty-two, from the highest levels of society. Pamphlets explaining the school's many benefits included instruction in French, Italian, and German, lessons in deportment and etiquette, music and painting classes, and every other skill a young lady of the *ton* required to make her debut and to catch the eye of the noblest, most respectable gentlemen. The school offered on-premises housing, particularly for young women whose parents were traveling abroad or who didn't care to venture away from their distant country houses. The modest uniforms which the young ladies wore may not have been particularly comfortable or fashionable, but they did give Miss Dobson's pupils the quaint appearance of schoolgirls half their age when they were marched across the street to the gated garden that stood as the centerpiece of Manchester Square.

But not everyone shared the same sunny view of the school as its founder.

"Has it occurred to anyone other than me that we are, in fact, prisoners?" Rebecca Burgess asked her two dearest friends at the school, Miss Josephine Hodges and Lady Caroline Pepys, as they made their obligatory circuit around the fenced garden.

"Prisoners are not tutored in painting with watercolors," Jo pointed out, hugging herself to block out the chill breeze swirling down through the stately, Georgian houses lining the square and rustling the leaves on the park's trees.

"Perhaps not," Caro said, "but you are aware that Miss Dobson sells the teacups and saucers we paint, and that she may or may not use the proceeds to line her own pockets."

"And she collected a fee from Lady Spencer when she sent the two Georgianas, Jane, and Elizabeth to sing at her soiree the other night," Rebecca added.

"I didn't know about that," Jo gasped. "She hired the girls out like trained monkeys?"

"She did," Caro confirmed.

"Ladies," Miss Dobson's shrill voice sounded from the center of the garden. The eyes of every pupil making their way around the perimeter of the garden as mandatory exercise paused to turn to her. "No giggling. You are to have uplifting, educational discussions only."

Across the garden, a cluster of young ladies straightened abruptly. Rebecca was certain she spotted Felicity Murdoch handing something to Lady Eliza Towers, who quickly concealed it.

"Oh dear," Caro said. "Felicity and Eliza are plotting again."

"Good." Jo breathed a sigh of relief. "Perhaps their antics will earn the rest of us a reprieve from evening recitations later."

Rebecca hoped her friend was right and that Felicity and Eliza were planning something. The only thing more tedious than boring meals of bland food in which no one was permitted to speak was the hour of reciting Bible verses that followed. Unless one of the pupils was able to distract Miss Dobson long enough for her to cancel the tedious practice and to send them all off to their rooms. Even though Miss Dobson insisted the recitations improved the wicked souls of the ladies under her charge, it was widely known that she would rather bustle her pupils off to their rooms in the evening so that she could enjoy a tipple of whatever hard spirits she'd been given by the parents of her pupils as thanks for keeping them out of trouble.

For as much as Miss Dobson attempted to advertise her school as an institution of refinement and perfection, the truth was whispered and giggled about at Almack's and at court. It was shared with sympathy and superiority when a young woman of good breeding went bad. And it was the most poorly kept secret in all of high society.

Miss Dobson's Finishing School was, in fact, a reformatory for young ladies who teetered on the brink of an utterly ruined reputation. It was the last resort of desperate parents—many of whom stood on thin ice with the *ton* themselves—to reverse the downward course of their daughters' fortunes. Miss Dobson—a former jade, but also the illegitimate daughter of a duke with close ties to the royal family—claimed to have turned sow's ears into silk purses and to have married several of her former pupils into the highest circles of the aristocracy. Or at least to social-climbing men of wealth.

"Stand straight," Caro whispered as she, Rebecca, and Jo continued their parade around the garden. "She's glancing this way."

"Look respectable," Jo hissed, shifting into perfect posture and putting on a bland smile.

Rebecca did her best to appear as innocent and stately as possible as she ambled slowly along the garden's gravel path. But it was no use. Miss Dobson glared at her, no matter what manner she adopted. The reasons were all too obvious. Miss Dobson had been present at Lord James Grey's house the night that Rebecca—along with her dear friend, Sophie Barnes—had posed completely nude and covered with sugar.

Rebecca still couldn't believe she'd been so scandalous. It had been Sophie's idea. She had discovered that Lord James Grey was a spy, selling secrets to the French. Worse still, Rebecca's own sister, Mary, had been in league with him. Rebecca had known that her sister and Lord Grey were involved, but part of her had assumed they were engaged in nothing more than the shocking sex acts she had witnessed the two of them partaking in through secret passages and voyeuristic spots that were built into the Burgess family house. Rebecca had received quite an education in carnality through watching her sister's congress with Lord Grey. But when it was discovered Lord Grey had dragged Mary into his traitorous deeds, Rebecca had joined Sophie's plan to bring him to justice.

Justice had involved quite a bit more sugar than Rebecca had anticipated. And far less clothing. Along with Sophie, she had stripped down to nothing, had the greater part of her body hair—including that in tender areas—forcibly removed with wax, and had splayed herself, covered in confections, on a table of sweets at Lady Charlotte Grey's engagement party. The ruse had worked. Lord Grey had incriminated himself in front of witnesses, including a Bow Street Runner, Mr. Nigel Kent.

Rebecca tripped at the thought of Nigel, stubbing her toe on a rock. Her cheeks heated. No, her whole body heated. The same way it had when Nigel had looked at her naked, sugar-covered body the night of the engagement party. His ravenous gaze had ignited feelings inside of her that had left her shivering and restless that night—

feelings that she wouldn't have minded the huge, hulking man sucking on sugared parts of her as though trying to drink the liquid center out of a chocolate.

"Are you quite well?" Jo asked, reaching out to steady her.

"Yes," Rebecca said.

Caro peeked sideways at her, a knowing grin tugging at the corners of her lips. "You don't look quite well to me."

Rebecca could feel her face heating even more. "I was merely contemplating the reason I am a prisoner at Miss Dobson's school," she said.

It was the truth. No sooner had Nigel brought her home, after Lord Grey's arrest had effectively ended Lady Charlotte's engagement party, than other Bow Street Runners had arrived at the Burgess home to question Mary. Rebecca had done everything she could to keep her sister from being implicated in the espionage— though she wasn't certain Mary deserved her help—but suspicion fell on her all the same. And on her parents. Nigel had managed to keep Rebecca from being caught in the same net by making clear to the authorities she had played an instrumental role in catching the spy, but the damage had been done. Mary had been shipped off to the Caribbean along with Lady Charlotte, their reputations in tatters. Rebecca's parents had taken the "opportunity" presented by the kerfuffle to travel abroad to Canada to visit her father's cousin. But before they went, they deposited Rebecca unceremoniously in the care of

Miss Dobson and her school, giving her strict instructions to forget everything that had happened, reform herself, and marry as dull a member of the peerage as would have her.

The prospect made Rebecca's soul ache in misery. The last thing she wanted to do was offer herself up on the altar of respectability to save her family's fortunes. She loathed the idea of shackling herself to whatever kind of man would be faultless enough to allow her parents to return to London on the merits of the marriage. Rebecca was repulsed by the idea of marrying any man when her heart—and a few more unspeakable parts of her anatomy—was captivated by one man and one man alone—Nigel Kent.

"You don't suppose my parents would consider anything less than an immaculate marriage to a member of the peerage, do you?" she asked her friends as they resumed their walk.

Miss Dobson was no longer looking in their direction, otherwise she would have censured Caro for laughing sharply.

"None of us are destined for the immaculate marriages our parents seem to think this bout of reeducation will afford us," she said in her usual, learned tone of voice. Caro was a bit of a genius, as far as Rebecca was concerned. She'd certainly read more books than her and Jo combined, which was part of the reason she'd been locked away at Miss Dobson's. Her parents had discovered that she'd been writing—and publishing—scandalous novels. "Reputations, once ruined, remain ruined," Caro said.

"I don't think so," Jo said. "Didn't Lady Alice end up marrying an earl upon completing her course of study here?"

"She did," Rebecca said, glancing to Caro to see how she would argue the issue.

Caro pursed her lips and arched one brow. "Alice had an arrangement with Lord Donnelly prior to being enrolled with Miss Dobson," she said. "An arrangement that was helped along by the alarming rate at which she increased in size shortly after beginning here."

Rebecca and Jo hummed knowingly in response. Lady Alice had only lasted a few months at the school before the futility of keeping her and Lord Donnelly apart had emerged. The ensuing wedding had been hasty and quiet, and the couple had removed to Lord Donnelly's home in Ireland with lightning speed, where his heir was born two months later.

"What about Miss Eloise Glenn?" Jo asked. "She was imprisoned—I mean, enrolled—at the school for more than a year before she caught the eye of Mr. Lewis."

"Mr. Lewis was a foreigner," Caro said. "An American. And the only reason Eloise agreed to marry him was because she heard that Johnny ran off and married a butcher's daughter in Norfolk."

"She cried for days," Rebecca remembered with a sigh. Eloise was the daughter of a newly wealthy shipping merchant and Johnny was a sailor that worked on one of his ships. Mr. Glenn had needed the marriage to solidify a trading alliance, thus Mr. Lewis.

Miss Dobson's school was filled with similar tales of illicit and unadvised love affairs, some that had been consummated, like Alice's, and some that had not, like Eloise's...and Jo's. Or so Jo insisted. Rebecca still wasn't certain what she'd done to land at Miss Dobson's. Only a few tales—like Caro's and Rebecca's own—had involved indiscretions of a unique nature.

"My point is that it is folly to think that condemnation to an institution that is known to harbor women of less than spotless reputation will result in acceptable marriages that will reverse a fall," Caro went on.

"But Miss Dobson promises otherwise," Jo argued.

"Miss Dobson is a pirate," Caro insisted. Her expressive mouth twitched into a wide grin. "Though I have to say I admire her originality and ingenuity."

Rebecca made a distasteful sound and glanced to the center of the garden, where Miss Dobson continued to stand like a sharp-eyed sentinel. She was exceptionally tall for a woman and built rather more like a Norse warrior than a delicate flower of femininity. Her figure might once have been pleasing, but now that she was in her sixth decade, she was rather solid. Her grey hair was pulled up into a style that may have been intended to appear soft, but still managed to look tight and forbidding with the harsh lines of her face under it. She glared as she studied her charges, ambling around the park like convicts set to work turning the gears of a large mill. She couldn't have appeared more forbidding if she wielded a whip and cracked it every time a group of pupils slowed down or whispered.

"Caroline Pepys. You cannot admire a battleax like that," Rebecca said.

Caro shrugged. "If all of us were as indomitable as Miss Dobson, we might not be here in the first place. We would be too busy conquering the world instead."

Rebecca laughed, but the sound only lasted a few seconds. Not because she feared Miss Dobson's wrath, but because a sudden commotion had broken out on the street just on the other side of the fence from where she, Caro, and Jo were walking.

A flood of men poured into the street from the house that stood just next door to the school. The neighboring house was owned by the East India Company, and while few of its residents lived there permanently, it was home to whichever trade officials needed a place to stay in London before taking to sea or returning to the subcontinent. The young women of Miss Dobson's school had spent more than a few hours pressing themselves to the windows in their pseudo-prison, gaping and gawking at the men of all descriptions who came and went from the East India House—dark men and light, Englishmen and Indians, those dressed in finely tailored suits and those wearing the exotic garb of cultures and religions that were as fascinating as fairy tales.

They were all rushing into the street from the East India House's front door. Rebecca, Caro, and Jo skipped off the path and pressed themselves against the fence as they watched the commotion. They weren't the only ones. Within seconds, half the young ladies of the school were clinging to the fence's bars to get a better look.

"Is it a fire?" one of them asked.

"Is it a riot?" another gasped, sounding excited by the prospect.

"Is that Lord Lichfield?" still another squealed.

A chorus of giddiness followed. Sure enough, Lord Lichfield hurried out of the house in close conversation with another man that Rebecca recognized as Lord Rufus Herrington.

"He's so deliciously wicked," one of the growing crowd of Miss Dobson's pupils that had rushed to the fence sighed.

Rebecca smirked. Lord Lichfield was wicked indeed. She'd heard from Sophie, who had heard from her sister, Honor, all about how the courtesans and actresses of London lusted after Lord Lichfield because of his unique talents. And while Rebecca still didn't understand what whips and riding crops had to do with the sort of things she'd seen her sister and Lord Grey engage in, that didn't stop half the rest of Miss Dobson's pupils from sighing and mooning over him.

"Girls!" Miss Dobson snapped, charging toward them at last, as Rebecca had known she would. "Get away from that fence at once. You are meant to be walking in peaceful contemplation of a moral and virtuous life."

The young women who had rushed to the fence

groaned and muttered complaints. Some peeled away from the fence willingly, but others stubbornly continued to look at the dispersing men. Rebecca was one of the latter. Something about the sudden flight of so many didn't sit right with her. There was no smoke so there couldn't be a fire. Why, then, did a dozen men of all sorts suddenly rush out into the street?

"What are you doing?" An Indian gentleman shouted as he, too, rushed out of the house, looking far more alarmed than the rest of the men. "Don't let them leave. One of them has the diamond."

"Diamond?" Caro said with a frown.

"Diamond?" Jo perked up, her eyes shining.

"Stop them," the Indian gentleman said as a few of the men—like Lord Lichfield and Lord Herrington—who had lingered near the house's front steps turned and walked off at a swift pace. "The thief is getting away."

"I assure you, he won't get far, Mr. Khan." Rebecca gasped as Nigel Kent marched out of the house and came to stand by the Indian man. Her heart did a loopy somersault in her chest and her skin broke out in prickles. "We'll catch the thief."

"But how?" the Indian man, Mr. Khan, lamented. "They're all getting away."

"We know the name of every man who was here today," Nigel told him. "The thief may have left before you made your announcement. We'll catch him yet."

"But the diamond," Mr. Khan pressed on. "It's worth a fortune, more than you can possibly comprehend."

"I will find it, sir. I give you my word," Nigel promised.

A flutter spread through Rebecca's heart...and lower. Nigel was every bit as heroic as she remembered him to be and larger than her memory had painted him. It had been months since the night of Lady Charlotte's engagement, months since they had sat side-by-side in a darkened carriage. She hadn't had time to dress properly, and only his clothes, a robe, and a thin layer of sugar had come between them. The heat between them in the carriage that night had been sweltering as she'd imagined the two of them in every sinful position she'd ever witnessed Mary and Lord Grey in. She'd even had half a mind to loosen the fall of his breeches so that she could fondle his male part the way she'd observed Mary doing. She would even have considered putting it in her mouth as Mary had done, which had seemed entirely distasteful to her up until that point.

Just as she was pondering the potential size of Nigel's member and what it would taste like, he glanced in her direction. Their eyes met, and a look of shock spread across his face. Rebecca caught her breath as Nigel excused himself from Mr. Khan and descended the East India House stairs to cross the street.

"Ladies, get away from there," Miss Dobson's shrill voice rang out from behind Rebecca. "Get away from there at once. This is unseemly in the extreme."

Rebecca gulped and turned to see how close she was to the certain doom of Miss Dobson catching her. To her surprise, at least a dozen other pupils were persistently clinging to the fence, smiling and waving and flirting with the men who had fled the East India House but who hadn't gotten far.

"This is an outrage," Miss Dobson continued to holler. "You will all be punished tonight. I will have you all kneeling on the stone floor of the classroom in nothing but your shifts, reciting verses while I smack each of your impudent bottoms with a switch."

"God help us all," one of the men fleeing the house groaned, grabbing his crotch in a decidedly ungentlemanly manner.

Rebecca hardly noticed the amorous reaction of a few men to Miss Dobson's threat, though. Her eyes were fixed on Nigel as he strode across the street, making his way directly to her.

"We'll distract Miss Dobson," Jo whispered by Rebecca's side, "but you must be quick."

Rebecca nodded absently as Jo and Caro pulled away from the fence, likely to cause as much trouble as they could on Rebecca's behalf.

"Lady Rebecca," Nigel greeted Rebecca as he reached the fence, touching the edge of his cap. "What are you doing here?"

"I could ask you the same," Rebecca said.

"A diamond has been stolen from a prominent minister of the Mughal emperor," Nigel explained in a rush, glancing to the side as though he shouldn't have been sharing the story. "It was meant to be a gift to the king to secure an alliance. Tonight's gathering was a prelude to the presentation ceremony, but when the diamond's case was opened, it was empty."

"But why are you here?" Rebecca instantly pinched her eyes shut, ashamed that she was handling their meeting so clumsily, then opened them, clinging to the fence with both hands.

"I and several of my colleagues were asked to provide security for the evening," Nigel explained. He blew out a breath. "Now it seems I'll be investigating a theft. But at least I know the culprit was one of the men present tonight."

He glanced down the street at the dispersing men who had rushed out of the East India House. Rebecca's heart ached for him. It must have felt as though he was watching any hope of quickly catching the thief slip away. Just like she had felt her chance to know him better slip away when he'd dropped her at her family's house the night of Lady Charlotte's engagement party and driven away.

"It's so good to see you again," she said, her heart brimming with pathos over what could have been.

"Likewise," Nigel said, his dangerous expression melting to a smile that was almost shy and definitely alluring. "I tried to come see you after...that night, but within days, your family's house was deserted."

Rebecca huffed out a breath. "I know, and I'm sorry. Everything happened so quickly after Lord Grey was arrested. Mary was shipped off to the Caribbean with

Lady Charlotte and I was unceremoniously deposited here."

"Where is here?" Nigel asked.

Rebecca opened her mouth to explain everything but was cut off by Miss Dobson's shout of, "Rebecca Burgess, if you do not come away from that fence this very minute I will switch you so hard you won't be able to sit for a week."

Nigel's expression went dark—both with anger and something far more tantalizing. "You'd better go," he said in a low growl.

"But we have so much to talk about," Rebecca protested.

Nigel closed one of his giant hands over hers as it clutched a slender, iron fencepost. "Meet me tomorrow at Hyde Park Corner," he said. "I won't be able to get away until four in the afternoon, but nothing will keep me from you."

"But, I—"

"Lady Rebecca Burgess!"

Rebecca whipped around only to find Miss Dobson only a few yards away, closing in on her.

"Go," Nigel whispered, letting go of her hand and stepping away.

"But, Nigel, I—" Rebecca tried again, but it was too late.

"I told you to get away from there," Miss Dobson said, clapping a hand over Rebecca's shoulder and forcing her away from the fence. "That will be bed without supper for you, for all of you. After all the sacrifices I've made to teach you young ladies to be better than your wicked natures, this is the thanks I get. I am outraged."

Rebecca had no choice but to let Miss Dobson drag her away from the fence and from Nigel. Nigel had already returned to the East India House and was whispering something to Mr. Khan anyhow.

"I am livid," Miss Dobson went on. "I am insulted. I am locking every one of you in your rooms tonight."

Rebecca's shoulders dropped, and she let out a sigh. How could she possibly dash off to meet Nigel at Hyde Park Corner the next day—as every bit of her longed to do—when she was locked away in her prison masquerading as a school?

CHAPTER 2

"This is an outrage," Caro said, arms crossed, as she paced the short length of the bedroom Rebecca, Jo, and Caro shared that evening. "My father does not pay Miss Dobson an obscene amount of money for me to be locked in my room like a disobedient child."

"Are you certain that's not precisely what he does pay for?" Jo asked in a small voice from where she sat on her bed. "I'm sure that's why my parents sent me here."

Rebecca sent Jo a sympathetic smile from where she sat on the sill of the room's one window, which looked out into the mews in back of the school. She still wasn't entirely certain what indiscretion Jo had been sent to the school to atone for, but, like Rebecca, Jo had heard nothing at all from her family—no letters and no occasional parcels of home comforts, like other girls sometimes received—since arriving.

"There are times I feel as though I was planted

18

here the way medieval prisoners were sealed in an oubliette," Rebecca sighed. "I would do anything to be free."

She turned and glanced over her shoulder out the window at the darkened mews, imagining Nigel was there, watching the East India House in an attempt to catch the diamond thief, but also keeping watch over her. If she could have, she would have jumped from the window into his waiting arms.

"That was a peculiar sigh for someone contemplating a life of imprisonment," Caro said, pausing in her pacing to grin wryly at Rebecca. "Does it perhaps have anything to do with the alarming gentleman with whom you spoke this afternoon?"

Rebecca turned back to her friends, blushing. "Perhaps."

Jo jumped off the bed and rushed to Caro's side as the two of them faced her. "Do tell," she said. "He was quite startling in appearance."

Rebecca's face felt hotter as she stood. "His name is Mr. Nigel Kent," she explained. "He is a Bow Street Runner who helped with the investigation of Lord Grey's treachery last spring."

She hoped to leave the explanation there, but Jo and Caro positively brimmed with excitement, their wide eyes fixed on her.

Rebecca let out a breath of resignation and went on to say, "He was of great assistance to me after Lady Charlotte's engagement party."

"The party where you and Miss Sophie Barnes posed nude?" Jo whispered, clapping her hands to her mouth.

"Yes," Rebecca squeaked. Embarrassment and the memory of that night had her as hot as a furnace. "We enjoyed an...interesting carriage ride back to my parent's house."

"Did he compromise your virtue?" Caro asked, unable to contain her grin. "Tell me what he did to you. Did he touch you inappropriately? Did you kiss? Did he stroke you into a tremor of ecstasy?"

Rebecca's mouth dropped open. Not for the first time, she wondered how Caro knew about such things. She wondered what kind of experiences her friend had had. Caro had been interred in their current mausoleum for writing inappropriate books, but Rebecca had never read one. She now wondered how her friend had researched the topics about which she wrote.

"It was nothing like that," she answered, pressing the backs of her fingers to her cheeks to cool her face. "But it could have been." She slipped into a mischievous smile. "I so wanted it to be."

Caro and Jo clutched each other and giggled.

"I knew it," Jo said. "I just knew Mr. Kent had the look of a man in love about him."

"Love?" Caro snorted. "He had the look of a man who wanted to dip his wick in Rebecca's well is more like it."

Rebecca joined their giggling. "I would do it," she whispered, scandalized at her own loose morals. "I don't care how wicked it is. I've...I've witnessed such acts before." She lowered her whisper even more. "I've seen how pleasurable they can be for a woman, and I would gladly engage in such activities with Nigel. With my whole heart."

"Then we must make certain it happens," Caro said, the light of mischief in her eyes. A moment later, Caro's face fell, and Rebecca's spirits with it. "If only we weren't trapped in this dungeon," Caro sighed.

"I believe a dungeon is a room below ground, like Miss Dobson's wine cellar," Jo said, a look of dread splashing across her face. They had all heard stories about the wine cellar. "We are more akin to princesses stuck in a tower."

A flash of inspiration hit Rebecca. "Princesses in towers in fairy tales always manage to find their way out," she said. "Surely there must be a way to escape this room."

"If there is, we will find it," Caro agreed with a nod.

The three of them launched into motion. Jo rushed to the door, testing the knob and the hinges. Rebecca and Caro turned to the window, prying the heavy pane open.

"It's a long drop to the ground," Rebecca sighed as they both leaned out.

"Perhaps we could tie bedsheets together to make our descent," Caro suggested.

Rebecca pulled her head back into the room. "But if that fails, then we'll be stuck sleeping on beds with tattered sheets. I doubt Miss Dobson would allow us fresh sheets if she saw we ruined what we have now."

Caro stared flatly at her, as though she were a ninny for thinking more of her own comfort than their collective escape. "Then we'll make a ladder or rope out of some other material."

"Good thinking."

Rebecca turned her attention to the room around them. There was very little in the way of furnishings or luxuries. The room was plain, with no ornaments on the walls, no carpet, and only their three beds, a washstand, and a wardrobe. The beds were narrow and unadorned. Rebecca's bed was pushed up against the wall with the window, and the other two were squeezed against the opposite wall. The wardrobe took up most of the space against the wall opposite the locked door. Searching for materials that would help them escape out the window took all of a minute before they decided there was nothing.

"It's hopeless," Caro said with a frustrated sigh, sitting heavily on her bed. "Miss Dobson is a dragon who guards her hapless princesses well."

"There has to be something," Rebecca insisted. She moved to the side of the wardrobe, hoping to find some sort of rope or cord keeping it fixed to the wall. "I refuse to believe our cause is—"

She stopped suddenly as she leaned against the wall in an attempt to see what was behind the wardrobe. Something was there—something with an eerily familiar feeling to it. The room's only ornament was drab wallpaper with a faded, floral pattern that didn't match up where different panels had been slapped against the wall. But behind the wardrobe, the panels of paper seemed to match up even less. In fact, Rebecca spotted a wide gap between two sheets of paper. A wide gap and a small, almost unnoticeable notch in the wall.

"It's just like our secret passages," she gasped. She grabbed hold of the side of the wardrobe and attempted to pull it away from the wall.

"Your what?" Jo asked, rushing to help her.

"Secret passages," Rebecca said. "We had several within the walls of our house."

"You had secret passages in the walls of your house?" Caro stood, blinking at Rebecca with the light of literary inspiration in her eyes.

Rebecca's face heated all over again as she said, "How do you think I was able to witness so many carnal acts? It was as though the passages were specifically intended for voyeuristic intent."

"I've heard of such things," Caro said as she too grabbed hold of the heavy wardrobe in an attempt to move it. "They're not all that uncommon. And yes, they are designed so that illicit behavior may be observed and enjoyed."

Rebecca was spared having to detail exactly how much she had enjoyed watching her sister—in spite of her paramour being the traitorous Lord Grey—when they managed to scrape the wardrobe a scant foot away from the wall.

"If this is anything like what we have at home, the door will open inward," she said, smoothing her hand along the wallpaper to the notch. "That way, the hinges do not protrude into the room being observed and its occupants never know they are being watched."

She finished her explanation by slipping her fingers into the notch, finding what felt like a small trigger, and pushing it. Instantly, there was a click, and the wall came loose. Another push, and it groaned open.

"Good heavens," Jo gasped, then burst into excited giggles.

"Ladies, we have our means of escape," Caro said in a triumphant whisper.

"But where does it lead?" Jo asked.

"It must lead into the East India House," Rebecca said, squeezing between the wardrobe and the wall. "Someone bring a candle."

They leapt into action. Jo retrieved two candles in their holders from the washstand in the corner of the room. She handed one to Rebecca—who took the lead as they advanced into the secret passageway—and brought up the rear with the other.

The passageway was dusty and narrow, but Rebecca's experience told her that it wasn't unused. There were no cobwebs lining the walls, and although she was loath to look closer, she didn't feel detritus that could be animal droppings or remains under her feet. She inched slowly along the passage, checking the space in front of her carefully before taking steps. The school did indeed butt up against the East India House. The two buildings were essentially one. Every once in a while, Miss Dobson and her students would hear the hum of conversations or exotic music on the other side of the walls.

It was late as Rebecca and her friends made their way down the passage, but they could still hear the drone of conversation and other activity. They turned a corner, which led them deeper into the house.

"Where are we going?" Jo whispered as they went.

"There have to be other doors," Rebecca whispered back. "Our house has several that let out into—"

She froze, holding up a hand. Caro nearly tumbled into her. Jo managed to stop without throwing them all into a pile.

"Is it a door?" Caro asked.

Rebecca waved her hand frantically for her friends to be silent. In the light of her candle, she could see small slits and handles in the wall that told her the purpose of that particular network of passages had the same purpose as the ones in her parents' house. There was no telling what they might observe if they slid one of the spying holes open. It was the sounds she heard that had grabbed her attention, though. She would know that kind of low, impassioned moaning anywhere.

She touched a finger to her mouth, then moved as silently through the passage as she could. The pleasured moans grew louder as they reached the end of the passage, near an intersection. There were two sets of moans, a man's and a woman's.

"Oh, my stallion," the woman sighed, then gasped as though she'd been touched in a particular way. "Yes. Yes, like that. Oh."

Behind Rebecca, Jo squeaked and slapped a hand to her mouth. Rebecca and Caro both turned to glare at her, and Jo shook her head in contrition.

"My little dove," a man's voice said, thick with passion. "Your cunny is as sweet as honey."

It was Caro's turn to snort, and to have Rebecca and Jo glare at her. Caro defended herself with a barely audible, "I cannot abide that sort of clumsy rhyme."

Rebecca gestured for complete silence as she leaned to one side then the other, attempting to ascertain which room the carnal activity was taking place in.

"Your thighs are like softened peaches," the man went on, followed by uncomfortably squelchy sounds. "I could drink your nectar all day."

The sounds continued as the woman's panting grew louder and more pitched. "My stallion," she yelped, sounding as though she were near climax.

"Your vessel is so precious that I should have concealed that diamond deep within your quivering walls," the man went on.

Rebecca had to swallow her gasp. She whipped to face her friends, mouthing the words, "The diamond?"

"Yes, my darling, you would have liked it if I had fucked you with that great, thick diamond, then left it buried deep within you," the man continued as the woman's mewling grew desperate. "Then you could have walked right out of here under that bastard, Khan's, nose instead of all the trouble I had to go through."

The woman evidently didn't care one bit what her companion was revealing. She moaned and gasped with complete abandon. Rebecca, on the other hand, could hardly keep still as a different kind of excitement surged through her. The diamond thief was on the other side of the wall. He'd confessed everything without knowing it. All Rebecca had to do to solve the case that Nigel had just begun to investigate was to find the right peephole.

She raised her candle and searched for handles on the wall, her heart pounding in her chest. As soon as she found one at her height—most of them were several inches above her head, as though meant for use by men or women of greater height—she handed her candle to Caro and slowly slid the panel to the side.

Her heart caught in her throat at the sight that met her, and her body flushed with heat. The room she now peeked into was decorated in an exotic, Indian style. Rich textiles and erotic art adorned the walls. Several colorful, carved chests and cabinets lined the wall. The center-piece of the room was a padded, oblong piece of furniture that Rebecca could only describe as a chaise. The man and woman they'd been listening to were quite busy using it for the purpose Rebecca assumed it was intended to serve, but that in itself presented an uncomfortable problem.

The woman was bent forward, almost as though in prayer. Her legs were spread wide as the gentlemen took her from behind. His movements were vigorous, which posed part of the problem. He bent so far over the woman as he tupped her that Rebecca couldn't see his face. Even more frustrating, the couple was facing away from the wall. The woman's skirts were thrown over her head, thoroughly concealing her identity. The only bit of the man that Rebecca had a clear view of was his finely sculpted backside as it pushed and flexed at a punishing pace. His breeches were loose around his knees and his shirt covered the rest of his body. The only distinguishing characteristic Rebecca could make out was a birthmark on the man's right cheek in the shape of a half moon.

Rebecca pulled away from the peephole, quickly scanning the narrow passage to determine if there were more points of observation that would afford them a view of either participant's face. What she saw were Caro and Jo with their faces pressed up against the wall. Jo was so enthralled with what she saw that her candle tipped farther and farther to one side, dripping wax to the floor.

"Jo," Rebecca hissed.

Her call had the opposite effect than what she'd hoped for. Jo jerked straight, dropping her candle in the process. The resulting clatter was followed by a strangled cry from the man in the room.

"What was that?" the woman asked in a muffled voice.

Rebecca gestured for her friends to flee as fast as they

could. Caro snapped her peephole closed and slid the panel concealing Jo's into place as well. Jo bent to scoop up her fallen candlestick, and as soon as she had it in hand, the three of them retreated down the passageway as fast as they could.

Rebecca was hardly aware of anything until they squeezed their way out from behind the wardrobe in their room at the school. Panting and terrified, they closed the passageway door and pushed the wardrobe back into place. Even then, the three of them leaned against the wall, ears pressed to the wallpaper, anxious to hear if they'd been followed. Blessedly, the walls were silent.

"Do you think whoever that was knows about the passages?" Jo asked, still whispering.

"There's no way to tell," Rebecca said. "Either way, they didn't follow us."

"Can you be sure?" Caro asked, stepping away from the wall and collapsing onto her bed. She was covered in a light layer of dust and her hair was disheveled.

Rebecca moved away from the wall, brushing her skirts and hair as well. "They would have caught us by now," she said.

"I don't know how I would even begin to explain what I saw if they do find us and question us," Jo said, her eyes wide and glassy, as she retreated to her bed. "That was...." She didn't seem capable of finishing.

"That was nothing compared to what my sister and Lord Grey would do," Rebecca said with a sudden grin.

She shook her head and pushed that part of what they'd witnessed aside. "More importantly, that man is the diamond thief."

"Agreed," Caro said. "But who was he?"

"I didn't get a good look at his face," Rebecca admitted. "Just his ass."

"I saw it too," Jo said. "He had a birthmark shaped like a half moon."

"More like a full moon, if you ask me," Caro added with a smirk.

Rebecca couldn't help it. She dissolved into laughter, sinking onto her bed and clutching her sides as the humor of the situation hit her. "How utterly ridiculous."

"It is, rather." Caro joined her in laughter.

Jo broke down as well, and in no time, the three of them were rolling on their beds. But Rebecca still felt the press of urgency where the diamond was concerned.

"Nigel has to know about this," she said. "I have to find a way to tell him."

"Agreed," Jo said, pushing herself to sit straight. "But what can you say? That the diamond thief has a birthmark on his bum? Surely your Nigel won't gather up all the suspects and demand they lower their breeches and present their bottoms for inspection."

Caro drew in an excited breath. "A whole line of men presenting their bottoms." Her cheeks flushed and her gaze turned dreamy.

Rebecca cleared her throat, bringing Caro back to earth. "Nigel should be able to do something."

"And truly, we know more than just the birthmark," Caro went on. Rebecca and Jo glanced questioningly at her. "The man was English," Caro said. "His bottom was deliciously pink. Or if he was Indian, his nether region was decidedly fair."

"And he was young," Rebecca said, excited by the details she hadn't realized she'd caught. "That was not the bum of an old man. He was too vigorous for age as well."

"But we couldn't see his hair," Jo said disappointedly. "He could have been blond or brunette or ginger for all we know."

"And his shirt was too ordinary to say if he was wealthy or poor." Caro deflated as well. "I wish I had thought to look for his jacket. That would have told us more."

"We know quite a bit," Rebecca said. "And that information needs to be conveyed to Nigel."

"But how can you reach out to him when we're trapped here?" Jo asked.

Rebecca chewed her lip and thought about it for a while.

"If only we had friends on the outside," Caro sighed.

Inspiration struck Rebecca, and she sat straighter. "We do," she said. "I can write to my friend Sophia. We aren't barred from writing to our friends. Sophia will be able to get a message to Nigel."

"That's a splendid idea," Jo said, clapping her hands. "Huzzah for still having friends in the outside world."

A twist of pity struck Rebecca. She was lucky in that regard. The Barnes sisters were her friends, and she was certain she could rely on them. As far as she knew, Jo and Caro had no one.

"I shall write to Sophie first thing tomorrow, as soon as we are let out of our cages. Sophie will know how we can contact Nigel, and once we do, we will help him catch this diamond thief.

CHAPTER 3

Sophie was a savior. Or to be more precise, her sister Verity was. Rebecca sent a letter to Sophie by special courier before the school's drab breakfast of lukewarm oatmeal—without any sugar—was finished, and a mere two hours later, as Rebecca, Jo, and Caro were dutifully painting flowers and woodland creatures on a never-ending line of teacups, an invitation to tea at the Marquess of Landsbury's house arrived.

"My, my," Miss Dobson said with a sniff as Rebecca put away her teacup art and started up to her bedroom to change into the one gown from the outside world that she'd been allowed to keep. "We must think very highly of ourselves to have such well-placed friends inviting us to tea."

Rebecca narrowed her eyes at the woman in loathing. It was clear she was green with jealousy that Rebecca had received any invitation at all. In all her time at the school, she couldn't remember Miss Dobson being invited to dine anywhere.

"I can't imagine why I'm being summoned to such a lofty home," Rebecca said, blushing furiously. She knew exactly why the invitation had been issued. If Sophie had followed through on the rest of the request Rebecca had made, Nigel would be at Landsbury House as well.

"Perhaps the Marchioness of Landsbury wishes to interview you for the position of scullery maid," Miss Dobson said, crossing her arms and looking down her nose at Rebecca. "Though I would not entrust you with even that."

"No, miss," Rebecca said, adding a facetious curtsy.

She darted upstairs and changed out of her uniform in no time, and was back downstairs, waiting on the school's front steps for the carriage Verity's note said would pick her up before she could catch her breath. The sense of freedom that came with being allowed out of the school, even if it was for just one afternoon, sent Rebecca's pulse pounding. It would be glorious if she could leave and never come back, if she could strike out on her own and make a new life. A part of her was certain Nigel would support her if she tried. He might do more than support her, he might—

But no, her heart sank as cold reality doused her, even as the cheery autumn sun of Manchester Square bathed her. Nigel was a Bow Street Runner. His life was most likely filled with danger. And while that didn't bother her in the least, it was also likely that he had very little money as a result. He'd always dressed casually when she'd seen him, and subtle hints about the length of his hair and the stubble on his chin hinted that he didn't have a valet caring for him. Could he even afford a wife? She didn't mind the prospect of slipping down a few notches on the social ladder, but if she was going to do such a thing, she would need to acquire far more skills than painting teacups, speaking French, and playing the pianoforte. She would—

"Oh, Mr. Hobbs, you are too kind."

The hair on the back of Rebecca's neck suddenly stood up at the sound of Miss Dobson thanking the green-grocer. She twisted to the alley that led to the mews behind the school just as Miss Dobson and Mr. Hobbs stepped out onto the sidewalk.

"Always a pleasure doing business with you, Henny," Mr. Hobbs said, tipping his hat.

It wasn't the forward way the grocer treated Miss Dobson or their sudden appearance that had caused such a reaction in Rebecca, it was the pitch of Miss Dobson's voice, the flirtatious lilt to her words. It sounded familiar. Strikingly familiar. Like a certain mystery woman she, Jo, and Caro had observed in a scandalous position the night before. But it couldn't be. Miss Dobson had been marching about the school, locking pupils in their rooms and threatening them with dire bodily harm if they so much as made a peep. Although if she were honest, Rebecca hadn't heard the woman shouting threats in the hall for a good while before she and her friends had commenced their mission in the secret passage.

She didn't have time to contemplate the odd situation further. A carriage with the Landsbury coat of arms pulled up in front of the school and the door opened.

"Good," Verity said from the carriage's luxuriously appointed interior. "You're waiting. I won't have to enter that awful school to fetch you."

Rebecca was glad as well. She skipped down the front stairs and flew into the carriage, hoping that Miss Dobson was too busy with Mr. Hobbs to take any note of her departure. As soon as she was inside and seated beside Verity, she let out a breath of relief.

"Thank you so much for helping me, Miss Verity. Or, no, I should call you Lady Landsbury now," Rebecca said.

Verity laughed with such happiness that Rebecca couldn't help but smile along with her. "I have no use for stuffy formality," she said. "Call me Verity and be done with it."

"Thank you," Rebecca said.

Verity Manfred was a sight to behold. She was vastly pregnant with her first child, but that hadn't stopped her from wearing a diaphanous gown in the latest and most scandalous, French style. The neckline scooped so low over her pregnancy-expanded breasts that Rebecca couldn't help but gape in the fear that, with one strong jolt of the carriage, they would pop out entirely.

"They are amazing, aren't they?" Verity giggled in

response to Rebecca's staring, taking hold of her breasts. "Thomas certainly enjoys them these days, although the alarming amount of tenderness this increased size has brought with it has killed some of the joy for me."

If anything, Rebecca gaped harder. No one in her entire life had spoken so freely and openly about such things. It was somehow even more shocking than spying on her sister and Lord Grey *in flagrante*.

"I wager that you'll find yourself in this delightful condition in no time," Verity went on, carrying the entire conversation as though she didn't have a care in the world. "Mr. Kent was devilishly eager to accept my invitation to tea this afternoon." Her eyes held a distinct sparkle and she couldn't hold her mirth inside.

"I have so much to tell him," Rebecca found her voice at last. "My friends and I may have discovered something of vital importance to Nigel's investigation of the theft of a precious diamond last night."

"I heard about the stolen diamond," Verity said, glowing with excitement. "Tell me more."

Rebecca spent the remainder of the short journey spilling out everything that had happened since the previous afternoon. Verity seemed particularly interested in the secret passageway connecting the school and the house owned by the East India Company. By the time they reached Landsbury House, both women were buzzing with excitement about all of the possibilities the theft, the investigation, and Rebecca's discoveries implied.

"Do you know," Verity said as they alighted from the carriage and made their way into Landsbury House's front hall, "I think I rather like your friend Caro's fascination with an entire line of men dropping their breeches simultaneously. I must have her for tea sometime. Perhaps I could ask the footmen to provide a suitable display."

Rebecca was about to reply that Caro's sensibilities didn't need that sort of validation when she turned the corner into a sitting room and nearly ran headlong into Nigel.

"Oh," she exclaimed as Nigel caught her to keep her from spilling to the floor. Rebecca's senses ran riot as she gazed up into his eyes. The heat from his muscular body seemed to cut right through the thin muslin of her gown. Or perhaps that was the sudden flush that pulsed through her. "Nigel," she sighed his name in greeting.

"Lady Rebecca," Nigel replied, slightly more formal, but still charged with attraction.

Verity cleared her throat. "I can see when I am not needed. I'll leave the two of you to discuss your diamond case in peace. Besides, I am in dire need of a chamber pot, thanks to this little bundle of joy." She rubbed her hands over her large stomach.

Before Verity departed, she reached into nearly concealed pockets on either side of the doorway and drew out sliding doors. They closed in the center with a click that left Rebecca and Nigel secluded in the parlor and sent Rebecca's pulse soaring.

For a lingering moment, silence reigned as Rebecca stared up into Nigel's warm, dark eyes. She forgot where she was and why she was there. All she could think about was the night Nigel had taken her home after Lady Charlotte's party, the way her skin had tingled from his touch and her heart had felt as though it would burst from her chest. She'd thought the tingling was due to her state of undress and the sugar covering her body, but as she stood there in Verity's parlor, the tickling sensation was back. It made her want to shimmy out of her clothes and ply herself against Nigel's body.

"You look well, Lady Rebecca," Nigel said at last, clearing his throat and taking a step back.

Rebecca's heart squeezed at the loss of his warmth. "You can call me Rebecca," she said, stepping with him when he moved toward the sofa closer to the room's cheerfully crackling fire.

"Are you certain?" Nigel asked, inviting her to sit.

"Of course." Rebecca sat. When Nigel took a seat at the other end of the sofa, she scooted closer to him. "And I hope you don't mind if I call you Nigel."

Nigel cleared his throat again and shifted uneasily in his seat. He tugged at his jacket, attempting to conceal his lap. Men's fashion didn't exactly allow him to hide everything, though. Rebecca's heart galloped in her chest at the slight bulge in his breeches.

"Rebecca," he said, color splashing his cheeks. Her name sounded so sweet on his lips that she leaned closer to him, her gaze dropping to the fascinating line of his mouth. He cleared his throat yet again and said, "You've discovered something about the stolen diamond?"

Instantly, visions of the carnal activity she and her friends had observed flashed to her mind. But instead of the mystery couple entwined so passionately, she saw herself bent over, bottom in the air, while Nigel pleasured her from behind. Only, as much as she'd witnessed in the past, her mind drew a blank when it came to what it would feel like to be engaged in such activities.

Nigel squirmed beside her, which jerked Rebecca back into the present with a gasp. She lowered her head slightly, her cheeks on fire, and pressed a hand to her chest. The movement only served to draw Nigel's eyes to the modest neckline of her gown. He stared as though her bodice were as low-cut as Verity's.

To save her sanity and prevent her from forgetting everything, Rebecca blurted, "There's a secret passageway that leads from my bedroom at the school to the East India House."

Nigel's eyes shot up to meet hers, and a small frown creased his brow. "A secret passageway?"

Rebecca nodded, inspired to go on. "We discovered it yesterday when Miss Dobson locked everyone in their rooms. Jo, Caro, and I were desperate to escape, and in our search for a way to lower ourselves out the window into the mews, we discovered the passage."

Nigel gaped at her. "And it leads to the East India Company's house?"

"Yes," Rebecca scooted closer to him, resting her

hands on one of his massive thighs. "The passages must be extensive. We only went a short distance, but I could see it went on. My parents have such passageways in their house, presumably so they can observe—" Her voice gave out, both because she couldn't possibly bring herself to confess to Nigel, of all people, what she'd seen from those passages, and because it had suddenly dawned on her that her parents must have enjoyed engaging in similar, voyeuristic activity. They had routinely invited friends to stay the night.

She shook her head to clear away a thousand shocking realizations about the sort of people her parents were. "We saw people," she blurted. "A man and a woman."

Nigel's frown had deepened at the beginning of her explanation. "In a place like the East India Company's house, passages of that sort must have been designed to listen in on sensitive discussions and learn political secrets. Even private conversations containing vital information can be spied on if few people know those passages exist."

"We saw a man and a woman making love," Rebecca blurted, certain her face was as red as the Persian carpet under their feet.

Nigel's eyes went wide and his thigh twitched under her hand. "You...did?"

"They were talking about the diamond," Rebecca rushed on. "Or, at least, he was talking about the diamond."

"What did he say about it?" Nigel's expression turned serious once more.

Rebecca licked her lips. "He said he should have—" she coughed lightly, "concealed it in her cunny so that she could have just walked out with it instead of him having to go through all the trouble he did to remove it."

A fire that was both serious and sensual filled Nigel's eyes. "So the man confessed to being the thief?"

"He did," Rebecca said, inching closer to him. "Why else would he have said those things?"

"Who was it?" Nigel asked.

Rebecca let out a breath, her shoulders sagging. "We didn't see. He was facing away from us, and his head was lowered as he—" She ended with a gulp.

"The woman?" Nigel asked, his voice gruff.

"She was on her hands and knees with her skirts concealing her head." Rebecca didn't know what possessed her not to stop there, but she went on with, "Her hips were elevated and her legs were spread. The gentleman gripped her around the waist and was thrusting powerfully." She held his eyes through her entire description, feeling parts of her turn molten.

Nigel stared at her with an intensity that left Rebecca wriggling inside. It was like the night of the party and then some. Her breasts ached, and more than anything, she wanted to rid herself of her clothes. It was simply too hot to wear them. He must have felt the same way. The bulge in his breeches had grown considerably. He couldn't be comfortable like that.

And yet, he didn't do anything. Rebecca could feel intensity pouring off of him. She knew he needed something, needed to act. But he held perfectly still. A little too still. She was desperate to discover what kind of excitement might burst from him, if only he would give himself permission to act. If that meant she had to be scandalous, taking a lesson from her sister's book, and make herself into a harlot, then so be it.

"I didn't understand what he meant," she said, glancing coyly at him as she slipped one of her hands to the inside of his thigh.

"About what?" Nigel asked in a rough growl.

"Concealing the diamond," she went on, inching her hand toward the bulge in his breeches. "How would one place something so precious in a woman's secret place?"

She was certain that he would leap up from the sofa in offense, that he would admonish her, call her every manner of wicked name, and march from the room, never to see her again, as she closed her hand over his breeches. She knew beyond a shadow of a doubt that she'd gone too far, been too bold, and that he would reject her. So when he groaned in pleasure and closed his hand over hers, helping her to rub what turned out to be the hot, hard, and rather large contents of his breeches, she gasped.

She was just getting used to the erotic way he helped her touch him when he pulled her hand away.

"Damn me if I'm going to come in my breeches in less than a minute," he panted.

Before Rebecca could do more than open her mouth

to ask what he meant, he scooped her around the waist and drew her across his lap. He cradled her with one arm, reaching for the hem of her skirt. At the same time, his mouth came crashing down over hers. The force of his kiss parted her lips, and before she could get her bearings, his tongue invaded her mouth.

It was the strangest and most unexpectedly enjoyable sensation she'd ever felt, and she moaned in encouragement. His tongue slipped along hers, tasting her fully and making her feel as though she were completely at his mercy. He couldn't seem to settle on one way of devouring her. One minute his tongue was mating with hers and the next he nibbled on her bottom lip, teasing her with his teeth.

Rebecca didn't think anything could be more glorious. At least, not until she realized his hand had found the hem of her skirt and was sliding slowly up between her legs. A quick bolt of shock hit her, then gave way to the heated, heady feeling that he was going to do more than fondle her knees.

He did stroke the surprisingly tender flesh at the back of one knee, but only for as long as it took to push it to the side. His motion caused her foot to lose purchase on the far end of the sofa and for her entire leg to slip off the side. The result was that her hips opened as his hand continued its scandalous journey.

His mouth covered hers and his tongue played against hers as his hand reached her sex. It was a good thing his mouth claimed hers too, because she cried out with the pleasure his touch brought her. He absorbed the sound, matching it with a groan of his own as his fingers stroked her hot, damp flesh.

He broke away from her long enough to growl, "My God, you're so wet."

Senses overloaded, Rebecca could only answer with incoherent sounds, her hips twitching against the things his hand was doing. He kissed her again, making sounds of his own as his fingers slipped deeper into her folds. Her whole body began to tremble as he traced the entrance of her sex.

"This is how you insert something precious inside a woman," he said in a low rumble.

He circled the opening of her sex once more, then thrust one of his large fingers inside. Rebecca gasped at the sensation and tensed, her body arching into his touch. He didn't remain still inside her, though. He moved his finger in and out, stroking her inner walls in a particular way, and producing a flood of delicious sensation that had her begging for more.

He seemed to hear her heart's plea and added a second finger to his ministrations. That felt even better and left her aching for more. Her body resisted just a bit, hinting that some barrier would need to be breeched in order for her to be filled completely, but she was ready for it.

"Nigel," she sighed as he broke their kiss. He watched her with such intensity that she could only imagine it must give him pleasure to see her so thoroughly undone.

"Come," he told her.

The command loosened something wild and wanton inside of her, and when he thrust his fingers deep inside of her, using his thumb to stroke the aching nub that she already knew could produce remarkable sensations within her, she gave up and let the most powerful orgasm she'd ever experienced thunder through her. She cried out as her sex pulsed, squeezing his fingers inside of her.

Nigel grunted in response, moving his fingers to keep her convulsing for as long as possible. When her tremors slowed and the liquid warmth of completion had turned her body to jelly, he growled, "I can't hold back anymore."

He drew his hand out from her skirts and grabbed her waist with both hands. As if she were a rag-doll, he lifted her and brought her down, straddling his hips. With a quick movement, he bunched her skirts around her waist, then arched his hips as he fought to undo the falls of his breeches as fast as possible.

Even though she was overcome with the heat of orgasm, Rebecca instinctively knew what he was after. She gripped the back of the sofa behind him as he tugged at his clothes to free himself. At last, she felt his hot, hard length rub against her sex. She jerked her hips, biting her lip at the pleasure that coursed through her as she ground her clitoris against his cock. He grunted impatiently and grabbed her hips, and Rebecca knew the moment had come.

But the doors of the parlor slid suddenly open, and before Nigel could drive himself home inside of her, Lord Thomas Manfred stepped into the room.

All three of them froze. Rebecca's legs shook as she balanced over the tip of Nigel's swollen cock. Nigel held her hips and held his breath as his head whipped to the side, glaring at Lord Thomas. And for his part, Lord Thomas couldn't have looked more surprised at what he was seeing.

Lord Thomas recovered first. "Bloody hell. I'm sorry, Kent." He looked genuinely embarrassed as he took a large step back, reaching for the sliding doors. "I wondered why these doors were closed. A thousand apologies. Do carry on. Sorry. Sorry." His words grew quieter and quieter until the last apology was delivered in a whisper as he shut the doors.

Rebecca sucked in a breath at last, but she still couldn't move. Every part of her wanted to bear down and sheathe Nigel firmly inside of her, but she sensed the magic of the moment had passed.

She was proven right when Nigel cursed under his breath and undulated his hips to draw his cock away from Rebecca's sex. He pushed her firmly back, and Rebecca was forced to plant her feet on the floor and stand to keep from tumbling backwards. As she did, Nigel tucked himself into his breeches with a frustrated growl.

"Is that the end?" Rebecca asked, her breath still coming in shallow pants.

"It is for now," Nigel said, sounding supremely uncomfortable. He stood so fast, pain pinching his face, that Rebecca had to stumble back several feet. "Thank you for the information you've given me. I'm terribly sorry if I've offended you. I need to find a toilet."

Rebecca snapped her mouth shut in surprise at Nigel's lightning-fast rush of words. The last clipped phrase made no sense to her at all. Nigel zipped out of the room, his gait hinting that he was highly uncomfortable.

"Wait," she called after him. "I haven't told you everything. The man had a birthmark."

Nigel didn't so much as pause as he fled the room.

"You didn't offend me," she yelped, rushing after him as far as the doorway. "I liked it. I wanted it. I want to do more. Can we do more?"

But it was no use. Nigel disappeared around the corner, leaving her feeling prickly and overexcited, and without true satisfaction.

CHAPTER 4

*N*igel Kent paced back and forth across the confines of his cluttered office on Bow Street, unable to shake the energy that pulsed through him. Days had passed, and the Chandramukhi Diamond was still missing. Not that the thief would be fool enough to attempt to sell it so soon after stealing it. Even if he had, surely someone in the network of eyes and ears that stretched out over London would have whispered something about the sale.

It further irritated Nigel that he had a list of suspects, but no firm leads on any of them. Any one of the men who had been at the house owned by the East India Company could have had a motive for stealing a diamond as precious as the Chandramukhi. There was Lord Rufus Herrington, whose estate revenues had reportedly fallen off so precipitously that he had resorted to selling his family's art collection in order to pay his servants. Then there was Mr. Wallace Newman, a mill owner from the north who had come to London in the spring to drum up investors. He'd overextended his company's finances and needed cash fast to stay in business. There was also Lord Felix Lichfield, who had just had his engagement to the elegant and high-placed Lady Malvis broken off for unknown reasons.

Those were only the English gentlemen who had been present the afternoon of the theft. Any one of Khan's Indian staff or guests could have been responsible as well. Although it was likely Rebecca would have noticed if the man who had confessed to the crime was Indian.

His pacing stopped abruptly and his thoughts flew back to the afternoon before. A hot rush shot through him, tightening his trousers. He'd been within inches, literally within inches, of driving himself home in Rebecca's hot, wet quim. She'd been biddable and pliable, and he had no doubt that she would have let him fuck her until they were both sore. She certainly would have been. He had no doubt she was a virgin, despite how readily she let him pleasure her. She was still intact, although maybe slightly less so now, after what his fingers had done.

He groaned at the memory, walking back to his desk and sitting hard in his chair with his legs splayed to relieve some of the pressure on his cock. He'd suspected Rebecca had a wanton streak in her from the moment they'd met. She might have claimed to be nervous the night Grey was apprehended, but he'd watched her as she posed on the sweets table. The way she'd held her body, large, heavy breasts thrust forward, thighs twitching ever so slightly, had been a dead giveaway.

She'd been lively in the carriage as well, sitting closer to him than was proper. It'd been all he could do not to ravish her that night, as the carriage bumped along the dark streets of London. He would never forget the scent of her—sweet mingled with spice—or the way she'd glanced at him, as if waiting to be pounced on.

He should have pounced.

"No," he grunted aloud. He shouldn't have pounced then and he most certainly shouldn't have taken the liberties he had with her at Lord Landsbury's house. He'd been raised to be more of a gentleman than that. But the way he'd behaved yesterday, anyone would have thought that he really was the raw, low-born scoundrel he was believed to be. His father would roll his eyes if he knew what a cad his eldest son had become. His mother had been rolling her eyes for years, ever since Nigel had left his birthright behind to be lowly thief-taker, as she liked to call it.

Which was why he should have been concentrating on finding the diamond thief, not reliving the way Rebecca had sighed with pleasure as he touched her silken cunny. His cock twitched with the rush of blood that the memory brought him. She'd wanted it and wanted it badly. He'd made her come and she'd reveled in it instead of being terrified of the sensations, as he imagined polite virgins would be. He closed his hand over his crotch, sucking in a breath and remembering the boldness with which she had done the same. Yes, she'd wanted it all right.

With a furtive glance to the door, Nigel undid the fall of his breeches and grabbed his cock. He let out a low grunt and closed his eyes, stroking himself slowly. The memory of Rebecca's gasp as she'd come filled him with a desperate sort of pleasure. He imagined what that moment would have been like if she'd had her tits out. He couldn't forget the sight of them that night at Grey's—full and round with large, dusky areolas. He stroked himself harder, pressure tightening his balls and heating his groin. He tugged a handkerchief out of the pocket of his jacket with his free hand, holding it ready.

His imagination flashed back to the day before. Rebecca had been so ready to be fucked. He could have sheathed his entire, substantial length deep within her. She would have taken all of him, no matter how tight the fit. He could imagine the way her face would have pinched with the effort, the impassioned cries she would have made as he stretched her to her limit. He didn't want to hurt her, but the idea that he would have been almost too much for her made him—

"Kent, what have you discovered about—"

Nigel's door flew open and his superior, Mr. Adolphus Gibbon, marched into the room.

Nigel flinched so hard, his hand clamping convulsively around his swollen cock—which was in full view, flushed, and tipped with moisture—that he let out a strangled cry of pain.

"Good Lord," Gibbon exclaimed, whipping to face away from Nigel. "Sorry to interrupt," he said, then, a beat later, hissed, "You're at work, man. Pull yourself together."

Nigel did just that, doing his best to tuck his thick, throbbing penis back into his breeches and to fasten them in some semblance of order before standing. "Sorry," he grunted, wincing at the harsh ache that begged for relief, but wasn't about to get any. "Unforgiveable," he muttered.

"I'm not against polishing rifles in general," Gibbon said, clearing his throat and peeking over his shoulder to make sure Nigel was presentable. "We all do it," he went on, turning gingerly to face Nigel once more. "But on our own time."

"Yes, sir," Nigel grumbled. Although he doubted Gibbon ever had to resort to self-abuse. The man was attractive in all the ways women liked—tall and fit, with dark hair, blue eyes, and a reputation for facing danger—both in his infantry days and now, as a Runner—that meant he never lacked for female company.

An awkward silence fell between the two of them. Nigel's groin pulsed with pain and desperation to finish what he'd started, but he gritted his teeth and stood at attention—in more ways than one—awaiting whatever Gibbon had barged in on him for.

Gibbon cleared his throat, then said, "I was going to

ask you what you've discovered about the Chandramukhi Diamond."

"Nothing new," Nigel growled. "Only that a witness may have heard the thief confess to the crime."

Gibbon's brow shot up. "A witness? Who? What did they hear? Who is the thief?"

Nigel swallowed, praying the conversation would be over as quickly as possible, before his balls fell off. "A student at Miss Dobson's School, the building that adjoins the house owned by the East India Company," he said. "But she did not see the man's face. She only heard his confession."

"When?" Gibbon took a half step forward. "Where did she hear it?"

Nigel hesitated. His protective instinct was to keep Rebecca out of the center of things as much as possible, but he couldn't withhold information from his superior. "A Lady Rebecca Burgess heard the confession through the walls of the house," he said. It was true without implicating Rebecca or her friends for trespassing in any way. "The confession was heard the day before yesterday. She did not see the gentleman's face." He didn't have to tell Gibbon why.

Gibbon frowned and rubbed his chiseled jaw. "The thief was in the house the day before yesterday," he said as though thinking. He hummed, then shook himself out of his thoughts. "If he is so bold as to return to the scene of his crime, perhaps he'll be there again tonight."

"Tonight, sir?" Nigel asked.

"We've received information that the East India Company is hosting a bacchanal tonight," Gibbon went on. "It's just the sort of ribald entertainment that a diamond thief would enjoy thoroughly. As I understand it, most of the key suspects will be in attendance."

"They will?" Nigel's brow shot up.

"Yes, and as it happens, I've secured an invitation for you as well," Gibbon went on. "You are to attend tonight's revelries discreetly and to observe our key suspects."

"Yes, sir," Nigel said with a nod.

Gibbon turned to go. "You can pick up the invitation in my office. There is time still before you need to leave to prepare so—" he smirked before stepping into the hall, "—carry on with your previous activity."

Nigel didn't have time to reply before Gibbon shut the door. He heard the man's laughter ring in the hallway as he walked away. That was enough to wither any lingering need he had within him. He sighed and sat against the side of his desk. There was nothing to do but to follow orders and attempt to nab the thief at the revels that evening. And if he was lucky, he would see Rebecca again as well.

"Have you seen the costumes that the gentlemen entering the East India House tonight are wearing?"

All it took was Lady Miranda Pope's loud question

echoing across the dining room at Miss Dobson's school
for a near riot to occur. Within seconds, half the girls at
the two, long tables had leapt to their feet to rush to the
windows that looked out on the street.

"Girls, sit down at once," Miss Dobson shouted over
the sudden chaos. She stood and rapped the serving
spoon she'd been using to dole out weak soup against the
table.

It was no use, though. Rebecca, Jo, and Caro leapt up
along with the others, rushing to the window. Caro
managed to wedge her way to the front and called back,
"It looks as though they're having a fancy-dress party.
They're all wearing masks and cloaks."

Another vocal thrill of excitement passed through the
room as the rest of the pupils jumped up to get a glimpse.

"This is an outrage," Miss Dobson shouted. "You will
come away from the windows at once and go to your
rooms, all of you. Miss Cade, Miss Conyer, Miss Warren,
get the other girls up to their rooms."

As was always the case in a place like Miss Dobson's
school, there were a number of girls who prided themselves on being loyal to Miss Dobson. Rebecca was
certain it was because the young ladies in question
delighted in bullying their peers and, in the case of Miss
Warren, physically pushing them whenever she had the
chance. Rebecca would have resisted the might of the
bullies and fought—like some of the others were doing—
to stay by the window. But after the discovery of the
secret passageway connecting their room to the Ease

India Company's house, Rebecca, Jo, and Caro were only too glad to be sent to their rooms.

"It isn't fair," Lady Miranda cried out as Miss Warren grabbed her arm and tugged her out of the dining room and into the hall, where Rebecca and her friends had already fled. "This is not a prison. My papa will hear about this."

"Your papa is a sour old lush who left you here to rot," Miss Warren informed Lady Miranda, who gasped and turned as if she would slap her.

As wickedly fun as it would have been to stay and see a fight, Rebecca had grander plans for the evening.

"We can sneak next door to observe the party," she whispered as she, Jo, and Caro raced up to their room. "Perhaps the thief is in attendance again."

"Do you think he'll reveal himself tonight?" Jo asked quietly. Other pupils had given up the fight and were returning to their rooms as well, although that could have been because their bedrooms faced the street.

"I would settle for the thief *exposing* himself once more," Caro said with a snort.

They giggled as they climbed to the second floor and slipped into their room. "You are wicked," Jo said as she shut the door behind them.

"Not as wicked as Rebecca," Caro said, arching a brow at Rebecca.

Instantly, Rebecca felt her cheeks heat. She'd told her friends about her rendezvous with Nigel in as much detail as she dared. They knew that she and Nigel had ended up alone, that they had kissed, and that there had been a bit of inappropriate touching. She hadn't been able to bring herself to confess the other wonderful things Nigel had done to her, though, and she certainly hadn't breathed a word about how close he had come to taking her virginity. The whole experience was still too new and too raw within her to speak openly about it. But she had spent the last two nights, long after Jo and Caro had fallen asleep, attempting to duplicate the delicious sensations Nigel had provoked in her. She'd managed to pleasure herself, but it wasn't the same. Not by a long shot.

"What do we do now?" Jo asked as the sound of more pupils returning to their rooms filled the halls.

"We wait until things settle down," Caro said, "and then we investigate."

As it happened, they didn't have to wait long. Within minutes, Miss Dobson made her way through the halls, shouting and raving about how horrid and ungrateful every one of her pupils was, and locking every door as she went.

"I wish she'd never discovered locking doors," Jo said with a sigh as the three of them sat heavily on her beds to wait. "It doesn't matter for us, but I feel sorry for the rest of the girls."

"Who knows?" Caro shrugged. "There might be doorways to the secret passages in some of the other rooms as well."

"If there are," Rebecca said, "I doubt anyone has discovered them yet."

They waited for some time more, until Miss Dobson had stopped raging and complaints had stopped coming from the other rooms on their hall. The entire school grew silent. Rebecca was tempted to draw a blanket around her shoulders and to nap for a while. As soon as that sort of weariness hit her, she knew it was time.

"Let's go," she whispered, standing. The three of them moved the heavy wardrobe enough so that they would be able to slip into the passageway. They each lit candles, but before Rebecca pulled the lever to open the door, she said, "We should branch out this time. We can explore just how extensive the passageway is and whether there are more exits if we split up."

"Isn't that dangerous?" Jo asked, her eyes wide as she lit her candle.

"No more dangerous than this entire enterprise is to begin with," Caro said with a shrug.

Jo took a breath and nodded, and Rebecca opened the passageway. Once inside, she started off in the direction they'd gone during their first trip. Caro headed off in the opposite direction, disappearing around a corner. Jo followed Rebecca for a few yards, then took a side passage that must have involved stairs that led to the floor below, since her candle quickly moved down in the darkness.

It was nerve-wracking being without her friends, but the sense of adventure and purpose that filled Rebecca was so potent that it pushed her on. She was filled with the same sort of giddy excitement that had filled her the night of Lady Charlotte's party. And the afternoon she'd spent with Nigel. Just the thought of him in combination with what she was doing had her skin prickling with excitement and her blood running hotter.

That could also have been due to the sounds of revelry she heard on the other side of the walls around her. In all directions, she heard laughter and music. She stopped at the room they'd observed the day before, sliding the panel aside to have a look. The room was empty. The chaise was draped with cloaks of all colors, and a table on the far side of the room held a basket that appeared to be filled with masks.

The spirit of adventure filled Rebecca further, and she brushed her free hand along the wall, looking for hinges. There had to be a way out of the passage and into the rooms of the East India House. If she could make it into that room in particular, she could—

Her hand brushed across a familiar-feeling switch and she pulled. With a click, the wall swung in. Rebecca held her breath and opened it wide enough to slip through. She searched the room frantically to be absolutely certain no one was there, and when she was sure, she dashed into the room, shutting the secret door behind her. Now that she'd crossed through it, she would be able to find it again.

Without wasting any time, she blew out her candle and set it on the table with the basket of masks. The sound of guests echoed through the halls, and a laughing man and woman even passed by the door to the room.

Rebecca snatched a mask from the basket and put it on as fast as she could. She grabbed a cloak from the pile next and clasped it around her shoulders to hide her drab school uniform. There were no mirrors in the room, but there was a window. She studied her reflection long enough to be satisfied that her identity was concealed, then skipped to the door.

For a moment, she hesitated. Was she truly ready to face the consequences of being caught, if that was what happened? She wasn't sure. But that merely meant that she needed to not be caught. What she had to do was find out more about the man who had stolen the diamond. There was no possible way she could go around tugging down men's breeches to look for a half-moon birthmark, but she could listen for the voices she and her friends had heard that night.

She darted out into the hall, holding her breath and looking around, uncertain where to go. That much was decided for her when a man turned the corner and started at the sight of her. He wore a mask shaped like a wolf and a silver-grey suit to match. A shock of ginger hair stood out around the edges of his mask.

"Well, well," he said in a wolfish voice. "I knew Khan was hiding treats in this part of the house."

"Is he?" Rebecca asked as the man came closer. She needed to prompt him into speaking more so that she could discern his voice.

"You look like a fetching little minx," he said as he prowled closer to her.

Panic filled Rebecca's gut. She couldn't tell if his voice was the one from the other day or not. It was unlikely that the first man she encountered in the house would be the thief. "I lost my way," she said as the wolf-man came closer.

"You most certainly did," he said, a growl to his voice. It was then that Rebecca noticed the bulge in his breeches. "Shall we step into this room to become better acquainted?" he asked, coming close enough to her to reach for her cloak.

Rebecca leapt away. "I'm looking for someone," she said, backing down the hall and hoping someone would stumble across them. She wasn't exactly frightened by the man. He certainly smelled delightful—like musky cologne. But after what she'd shared with Nigel, she had no wish to become better acquainted with anyone else.

"I'm not who you're looking for?" he asked, his mouth —which was visible under the bottom of his mask— turning down in a pout.

"No," she said, moving faster down the hall. "I'm looking for—" A flash of inspiration hit her. "I'm looking for a man with a half-moon birthmark on his bum."

The wolf-man laughed out loud. "What do you want him for? He's a cad and a bounder. And he only has half a moon, if you catch my meaning."

Rebecca thought perhaps she did. She couldn't help but giggle at the idea, in spite of feeling as though the wolf-man was stalking her down the hall. He would respect her refusal, wouldn't he?

Fortunately, she didn't have to find out. She reached the corner at the end of the hall and was overjoyed to find a staircase leading down. Better still, there were a great many people at the bottom of the stairs. She rushed down to join them, no longer quite as anxious as the wolf-man followed her.

But the moment she fled into a large, highly-decorated room filled with the scent of exotic spices, she had a bigger problem. Dozens of people turned to look at her. Two-thirds of them were men dressed in all manner of costumes, all wearing masks. The rest were women in various states of undress. Many wore gowns that were soaking wet and which clung to their bodies, hiding nothing. A few wore dry gowns, but had their bodices peeled down to expose their breasts. One wore nothing at all, but was bedecked in jewelry. A man whose mask had curling ram's horns protruding from it paid special attention to her, fondling the paste gems spilling across her chest as much as her breasts. About half of the women were Indian, but regardless of their national origin, Rebecca was certain beyond a shadow of a doubt that they were all harlots. They were the evening's entertainment.

All but one. For right there, in the center of the room, her sagging breasts fully exposed, a trio of older men leering at her, was Miss Dobson. Rebecca gaped at her. Not an hour ago, the harridan had been storming the halls of the school, locking her pupils in their rooms, and now there she was, already in her cups. She wore a half-mask made of green feathers, but there was no mistaking her wide, mean mouth. When one of the men circling her grasped one of her breasts and squeezed, Miss Dobson gasped and laughed.

Rebecca took a step back in shock, but the movement caused her to run smack into the wolf-man. He caught her around the waist, his hand reaching into her cloak and finding one of her breasts.

"Are you certain you're not looking for me?" he asked, squeezing her breast and grinding something stiff against her backside. "I'm hung like a donkey, you know," he whispered against her ear.

Rebecca shivered—not so much from fear, but because she suspected that, were it not for Nigel, she would have spread her legs for the man in a heartbeat. He smelled so good and was obviously fit. She refused to betray the man her heart wanted simply to satisfy her body's curiosity, though.

"I'm sorry, sir," she said, praying he would understand, "but I'm afraid—"

"Hold on," Miss Dobson called out, turning to Rebecca and losing her smile. She pushed her half-mask up to her forehead and squinted hard at Rebecca, or rather at her skirts. "Where did you get one of my uniforms?"

CHAPTER 5

*W*ithin minutes of arriving at the house owned by the East India Company, Nigel's list of possible diamond thieves began to narrow.

"Of course, Coleman swore he'd never return," he heard a pair of masked men—who were obviously the Duke of Westmoreland and the Earl of Derby—saying. "That ruddy diamond thief stole his gold watch right out of his waistcoat pocket in the frenzy after the Runners arrived."

"You don't say."

Nigel edged past the men, deeper into the small refreshment room across the hall from the ballroom, where most of the entertainment was taking place. That information matched what some of his colleagues had already discovered about Coleman. The sheer clueless-ness of Westmoreland and Derby was enough for him to cross them off the list of suspects, pending further investigation.

The true thief might very well have been present at that evening's entertainment, though. Nigel had a strong hunch that the thief hadn't just taken the diamond and run. The East India Company was too rich a target to strike once and vanish. He would have bet his inheritance that the thief was planning to strike again. Which meant he could very well be just around the corner.

No sooner had the thought popped into his head than the man who was helping himself to a cup of punch at the table where Nigel stood knocked over a bottle of spirits. The bottle tipped over, splashing amber liquid on Nigel's breeches.

"Sorry, friend," the man said scrambling to set the bottle upright. "How clumsy of me. I was just admiring that elephant-headed chap there." He pointed to a gold statue of the god Ganesh that sat on a small dais in the center of the table. A fat ruby adorned the statue's forehead. "How much do you suppose that's worth?"

Nigel's nerves bristled, and he glanced up at the man, narrowing his eyes behind his plain, black mask to study him. He could tell at once he was speaking to Lord Herrington, even though the man wore a mask in the shape of a wolf's head. His ginger hair was a dead-giveaway, not to mention the cut of his jaw and the way his mouth slanted in his tell-tale grin. Herrington was right at the top of Nigel's list of suspects. And he was pointing out the house's valuables.

"Are you in need of money?" Nigel asked, hoping bluntness would take Herrington by surprise and make him lax.

Herrington laughed. "Aren't we all?" He sighed and studied the statue once more. "I'm in need of something else even more though." He adjusted his breeches with his free hand. "Thank God Khan is footing the bill for the ladies tonight."

Nigel wanted to question Herrington further, but another man bumbled into the room. He wore a ram's head mask and shuffled straight to the punch bowl, where he poured himself two glasses.

"Bloody hell," Nigel muttered, wishing the ram's headed man would leave so he could interrogate Herrington.

Herrington finished his punch and put the empty cup aside. He nodded to Ganesh once more and said, "Khan should be careful about keeping that out. It's small enough that one could simply slip it in one's pocket and carry it off."

The ram's headed man jerked up to stare at Herrington. It was difficult to tell, but Nigel thought his eyes went wide behind his mask. "They'd notice," he grumbled, seemingly offended. "Of course, they'd notice." He snatched up the two cups of punch he'd poured, then dashed out of the room.

A second too late, Nigel recognized the man's voice and identified him—Wallace Newman, one of the other suspects high on his list. His stomach lurched, and he took a step as if to follow Newman. But then he hesitated. He wasn't finished with Herrington yet.

Herrington, however, was finished with him. He clapped Nigel on the shoulder and said, "The wolf is off to hunt, and I've seen quite a few tasty birds as prey. I hear the best ones are hiding upstairs. Wish me luck."

Herrington strode out of the room. Nigel followed him, fully intending to stop him and drag him aside for more questions. But he was stopped in the hallway by a man wearing a mask of eagle's feathers.

"Wait, I know you," the man said in a rich baritone.

Nigel was forced to stop, mostly because he recognized the man in return. "Lord Lichfield," he said with a slight, grudging bow. Yet another man high on his list. Perhaps all was not lost with Herrington's departure. "What brings you here this evening?"

Lichfield laughed. "The same as the rest of us." He shrugged. "Free wine, free food, and women who are free with their favors."

"You can't pay for all that yourself?" Nigel asked.

Lichfield's mouth quirked into a grin below his mask. "I certainly can, but it's not about the blunt, is it? It's about the thrill of the chase, the rush of excitement that comes from doing something devilish."

Nigel's pulse sped up. Perhaps Lichfield was the thief after all. Herrington was desperate for the money, but some men were wicked for the sheer thrill of it. Lichfield did have a certain reputation amongst the ladies. Perhaps this was another outlet for that addiction to the thrill.

"Have you seen what Khan has on offer?" Lichfield thumped Nigel on the back and drew him into the ballroom where the main activity of the evening was taking place. At least, the main public activity. "He's presented us with a variety of gems to choose from."

Nigel's senses flashed to the alert. Why would Lichfield use those words if he wasn't focused on jewels, on diamonds? "Very nice," he said, letting himself be immersed in the revelry.

The noisy, crowded room was filled with a hundred distractions—from drunken guests to sensual, naked women. Instinct gripped Nigel at the sight of so much exposed flesh, and within minutes, he was semi-erect. He gritted his teeth and tried to scold his body into business, but after the intensity with which he'd been pining for Rebecca—and he wasn't too proud to admit he'd been pining, his cock had been hard as pine for days—he couldn't help but be aroused by his surroundings.

But he was there to work, not to lose himself in the pleasures of the senses. The thief had to be there. He ran through the list of suspects in his mind as he took up a position close enough to the door that he'd be able to spot anyone leaving in a hurry but far enough away that he wouldn't appear menacing. Khan routinely invited all manner of society to his bacchanals. London was filled with scandalous revelries any given night of the week, but Khan's had a reputation for the exotic as well as for debauchery. They always drew an interesting crowd.

A particularly crude bark of female laughter caught

Nigel's attention, and he glanced across the room to find none other than Miss Dobson, the owner and headmistress of Rebecca's school, smack in the middle of the debauchery. His brows shot up, particularly when Miss Dobson slurred, "Well, if you say so, your lordship," and handed her glass of punch to one of the gentlemen crowding around her. She then proceeded to tug her bodice down until her flabby tits spilled over the edge.

Nigel grimaced, but the men leering at Miss Dobson seemed to like the display. Nigel made a note to investigate who exactly Miss Dobson was, why she owned a so-called school that was little more than a holding-pen for women of large fortune who had gotten into trouble, and why Khan had invited her to his festivities.

He took one step toward Khan—who was holding court at the other end of the room with a certain set of bare-breasted, blonde twins with a reputation for debauchery that made even Nigel pale—when Herrington returned to the room. It wasn't Herrington's return that froze him in his tracks, though, but rather the woman who had rushed into the room right before him.

"Rebecca?" he muttered. His pulse pounded, and his half-erection started toward a full one. She was obviously out of place, dressed as she was, but her mask seemed to hint that she was there to participate. Nigel's gut tensed with rage as Herrington sidled up behind her, reaching under her cloak and whispering something in her ear as he stood too close.

A split-second later, a few more pieces flew into

place. Rebecca couldn't be there to participate. She was still dressed in her school uniform. Even with a mask, he could see she was shocked by what she'd seen. She must have come through the secret passageway for some reason. But why would she—

"Hold on. Where did you get one of my uniforms?" Miss Dobson asked in a voice loud enough and sloshed enough to draw attention from half the people in the room.

"Is it?" Rebecca squeaked. "I don't know...I didn't... that is, I found it...."

"Let's get you out of that uniform," Herrington said, reaching for the clasp of the cloak at Rebecca's neck.

At the same time, Miss Dobson slurred, "I know your voice."

Nigel shot into action, a combination of anxiety and pure, unadulterated jealousy fueling him. He marched toward Rebecca and Herrington, blocking Rebecca from Miss Dobson's view.

"There you are," he said when he reached Rebecca. He scooped her right out of Herrington's arms as carefully as he could without causing a bruising tug-o-war. "I've been searching everywhere for you."

Recognition dawned in Rebecca's eyes as soon as she glanced up at him, and she breathed a noticeable sigh of relief. "You see?" she told Herrington, clinging to Nigel's side. "I told you I was here to meet someone."

"Lucky devil." Herrington backed away, his hands raised in graceful concession, but Nigel still felt like pounding the man in the face. Herrington winked at Rebecca behind his wolfish mask. "Let me know when you're done and I'll show you what a real man can do."

Yes, Herrington definitely deserved a bloodied nose. Nigel's certainty that he was the diamond thief grew. He sent Herrington a warning look before whisking Rebecca out of the room and around the corner to a secluded alcove.

"What are you doing here?" he hissed, careful not to be overheard.

Rebecca seemed to sense the need for secrecy. "I snuck over to see if I could learn more about the diamond thief. There's more that I didn't have a chance to tell you the other day. The thief has a half-moon—"

"Where did she go?" Miss Dobson's voice echoed from the doorway to the ballroom. "I swear I know her."

Nigel leaned into Rebecca, pinning her against the wall of the alcove and slanting his mouth over hers, both to stop her from talking and to shield her from Miss Dobson. His intent was purely defensive, but the moment their lips met, the need he'd been feeling for days welled up in him. It didn't help that Rebecca sighed and threw her arms around him without a moment's hesitation.

Sense and purpose fled as Nigel devoured her. He thrust his tongue against hers, taking what he needed so desperately. He wedged his knee between her legs, pinning her further and rendering her helpless. He planted one hand against the wall for balance, but slipped the other under her cloak to squeeze her breast. He would have ripped her high-necked bodice so that he could touch her bare flesh, but then Rebecca would have had to explain the damaged gown.

That suddenly rational thought, combined with Miss Dobson's continued complaint of, "I could swear she was one of mine, but they're all locked in their rooms. How could one of my charges be in attendance?" helped him to remember his purpose. As soon as Miss Dobson was whisked upstairs by two of her companions, Nigel straightened, panting.

"We need to go somewhere we won't be interrupted," he said, reluctantly letting Rebecca go.

Rebecca lurched forward with all the coordination of a wet rag. She sagged against Nigel, her eyes bright and her lips swollen and red. For a moment, the sounds that came from her lips were more pleading for them to resume their activity than anything else. They finally coalesced into words when she said, "Upstairs."

Nigel nodded. He grasped her around the waist and set her fully on her feet. A burst of laughter from the ballroom served to bring her fully to her senses, though. She swallowed, grabbed his hand, then hurried down the hall with him to the staircase, then up to the first floor. They climbed another flight of stairs to the second floor, then she tugged him down a hallway filled with rooms Nigel guessed were either where the East India Company's guest stayed before returning to the subcontinent or, judging by some of the sounds he heard, where revelers came to have a moment of privacy.

"In here," Rebecca whispered at last.

She led him into a small room with a chaise that was contoured specifically for carnal activity. The chaise was draped with cloaks like the one Rebecca wore, and a basket of masks sat on a table. It must have been a dressing room for guests who hadn't brought their own costumes. Rebecca took off her mask and cloak and snatched up a candle from the table with the masks, then crossed to what looked to Nigel to be a bare wall. But the moment she reached it and touched a certain spot, the wall swung open.

"Your secret passage," he said, following her into the dark, narrow space between the walls.

As soon as he was wedged into the uncomfortable space, Rebecca shut the door behind him. "Jo and Caro are in here somewhere," she whispered. "We all snuck in to see what we could find out. I found the cloaks and masks and figured I could find out more if I joined the rest of the party, but then that wolf man found me."

"Lord Herrington," Nigel growled.

Rebecca blinked in the candlelight. "Is that who he was?"

"He's a suspect," Nigel told her. "In fact, I'm convinced he's the thief."

She gasped and pressed a hand to her chest—a chest he longed to free from the constraints of her drab uniform and explore for hours. "No. I could have cornered him and questioned him."

Nigel chuckled dangerously. "I'm afraid he would have cornered you and done far more than ask questions."

Even in the dim light, Nigel could see her blush. "I'm not sure I would have been strong enough to resist if he had," she confessed. "I'm not a good girl."

A fierce rush of protectiveness pulsed through Nigel. If Rebecca hadn't been holding a candle in an impossibly narrow passage, he would have swept her into his arms. "You are good, Rebecca," he told her.

She shook her head. "I'm not. I'm very naughty indeed." Her voice took on a guilty, defeated tone as she went on with, "Good girls don't ache to feel a man's touch. Good girls don't constantly think about how it must feel to be used by a man, to have his cock inside of them. They don't daydream about what he must taste like."

Lord help him, she was going to cause him to spend in his breeches if she kept talking like that. And with such innocence as well. "There's nothing wrong with any of that," he said, well aware of how rough he sounded. "If you feel that way about the right man."

"I feel that way about you," she said, surging toward him. "I want to be your lover so badly that I can't sleep at night. I have ever since the night of the party."

It was pure torture, hearing her words and being physically trapped in a space where he couldn't act on it. "I want you too," he growled. "So badly that I've had a cockstand for days. I would have buried myself in your sweet pussy to the hilt the other day, if Landsbury hadn't interrupted us. I would have fucked you senseless, and then I'd've done it again and again."

"Ohh," she sighed, the sound shaky and filled with need. Her breath came in shallow gasps. "Oh, my. I—" She glanced around as if looking for a place to put her candle down so that she could jump him. "There has to be—"

Without finishing her sentence, she turned and darted off down the passageway. Confused and overly aroused, Nigel was forced to follow her or be left in the dark. She felt her way along the wall, sliding something aside now and then and, he assumed, peering into the rooms they passed. She hummed with a note of desperation, as though eager to find a room where they could go at it like rabbits.

Her humming stopped with an abrupt squeak as the sound of two male voices came suddenly through the wall.

"I tell you, I can't sell it yet."

Nigel instantly recognized the voice as Herrington's. Anger renewed in his gut, and he hurried silently to Rebecca's side as she peered into one of the rooms.

"I beg of you," Khan said. "I need this, for me and for my son."

"What does Saif have to do with all of this?" Herrington asked.

"He's as much a part of it as Lichfield is," Khan went on.

"Lichfield," Herrington snorted. "The man is a friend, but he's clumsy. He may have helped me acquire it in the first place, but he keeps dangerous company. Get the wrong woman involved and the truth will be all over London. We'll have that Runner all over us in no time."

"Him?" Khan laughed. "I wouldn't worry about him. His mind is elsewhere. Now, come along before we are missed."

Nigel flinched as Herrington and Khan left the room. Once he was certain they had gone, he growled and banged his fist against the passageway's wall. Half his frustration was for the revelations he and Rebecca had heard, but half was because now he couldn't possibly, in good conscience, do any of the things he had been planning to do with Rebecca just moments before.

She seemed to sense the truth of the situation they were in as well. "Oh," she squealed in frustration, sagging against the wall beside him. "This is wretchedly unfair."

"I know," he sighed, rubbing a hand over his face. "But now we know who stole the diamond."

"Is that what they were talking about?" She peeked hopefully up at him. "Couldn't we pretend we heard nothing?"

Nigel's mouth twitched to a grin, and for a change, it was his heart that ached for her. She was sweet, in spite of her insistence that she wasn't. She was cleverer than he supposed she gave herself credit for too. It infuriated

77

Nigel to think that her insistence that she was bad likely came from the way her family had treated her. He could offer her so much more than they ever had and would treat her better than she could possibly imagine.

"There's still time, isn't there?" she asked, her eyes round and hopeful and her cheeks flushed pink. "What if I clung to you like this?" She handed him the candlestick, then pivoted to stand with her legs spread on either side of his and began tugging up her skirts. "We could be quick about it."

Nigel's groin ached so badly that he wasn't sure he'd be able to walk normally for a week. "Rebecca?" he asked as she leaned into him, resting her hands on his hips. "Are you a virgin?"

She blinked, then nodded in shy affirmation.

That only made his heart beat harder. "Then I'm not going to spoil you standing up in a narrow, dusty, secret passageway in the dark."

"You're not?" She seemed genuinely disappointed.

He shook his head. "I'm going to take what I want from you in a bed, in broad daylight, when we can linger and enjoy ourselves, and when I can make you come at least half a dozen times before we're too exhausted to go on."

"Ohh," she sighed, her voice quivering. He could feel the tension rippling off her body, so close to his. "I think I would enjoy that immensely."

"I will promise you something else as well," he went on, amazed at his own powers of restraint, given the circumstances and her proximity. "I'll find a way to get you out of that wretched school. Even if I have to invent lies so that the hypocritical Miss Dobson will let you go. I'll say you're an essential witness in an ongoing investigation."

Rebecca straightened. "I am, though, aren't I?"

Nigel smiled in spite of himself, brushing the side of her face with his free hand. "You're essential in every way, love. I won't ever let you forget it."

"Nigel." She breathed his name softly, then lifted to her toes to kiss him. It was a sweet kiss, and he let her take complete control, even though his balls ached so badly he wanted to groan. He would wait as long as it took to find exactly the right time to make her his. And once he had, he was beginning to doubt if he'd ever be able to let her go.

CHAPTER 6

*I*t was pure torture for Rebecca to separate from Nigel in order to find Jo and Caro and to return to their room. But Nigel was right when he told her that between the walls of someone else's house was no place to make love. And it truly was important for him to track the diamond thief's movements. Nigel seemed certain Lord Herrington was the thief. In spite of what they'd heard, Rebecca wasn't as sure. It didn't seem quite right that a man who smelled so good and who had whispered so seductively to her could be guilty of stealing a diamond. Although she could certainly imagine him stealing a woman's virtue. Some *other* woman's.

"You'll never believe what I saw." Caro knocked Rebecca's thoughts on the matter clear out of her head as the two of them met at one of the passageway's intersections a few moments later.

"Wait, wait," Jo whispered, dashing up from the

direction Caro had come from. "Don't share anything without me. I have a few things to share myself."

The three of them crept back into their room, set their candles aside, and pushed the wardrobe back into place. Once it was secure and they all climbed onto Caro's bed to share their discoveries, all three blurted almost in unison, "Miss Dobson was at the party."

They collectively dissolved into shrieks and giggles, then spent a solid five minutes talking over each other about the scandalous things they'd seen their headmistress doing.

"Is it even proper to touch a man's member like that?" Jo asked breathlessly as they rounded up the discussion. "Let alone two of them at once."

"It's not proper," Caro said, a naughty glint in her eyes, "but it is revelatory. And I must say, as much as I loathe the woman, to have the dexterity to pleasure two men simultaneously is quite an accomplishment."

Not for the first time, Rebecca wondered what devilish deeds Caro had done to find herself enrolled at Miss Dobson's school. It had to be more than simply writing salacious novels.

"I think she knows something about the diamond," Jo blurted just as Rebecca opened her mouth to ask about Caro's past.

"What?" she and Caro exclaimed at the same time.

"I think she's involved with the diamond," Jo went on in a tight whisper, as though Miss Dobson were listening with her ear pressed against the door. She turned bright pink and said, "One of those men said something about —" she swallowed, looking a little sick, "—putting something in her, and she laughed and said he'd better hurry, because someone else had offered to put something far more precious up there."

Rebecca sat bolt upright.

Caro gaped at Jo. "It can't be coincidence," she said. "It's too close to—"

"—what the thief said the other day about the diamond," Rebecca finished the sentence for her. "Could Miss Dobson have been the woman we saw...." She let her words die. It was too horrible to think that they'd witnessed their headmistress in such a position. It was bad enough that Rebecca had seen her half undressed. She shook her head. "I have to let Nigel know about this."

"But how are you going to tell him?" Caro asked.

"He said he would find a way to get me out of the school," Rebecca went on, her face heating. "He was there, at the party."

She launched into the story of what had happened to her from the moment their merry band had parted ways... leaving out a few details that she wasn't quite ready to share yet. She did, however, share Nigel's suspicions about Lord Herrington and what he'd said to Mr. Khan.

She saw that conversation as a minor detail, until Jo jerked straighter and said, "They mentioned Lord Lichfield?"

"Yes," Rebecca said, studying her friend, who flushed a darker shade of pink. "Is it important?"

Jo swallowed. "I saw Lord Lichfield in one of those rooms. He had one of the ladies from the party bent over his knees, and he was spanking her soundly."

"Yes, I'm told that's what he does," Caro said with a giggle. "And more. Much more."

Jo's eyes went wide. "The woman didn't seem to mind, in fact—"

"What does this have to do with the diamond?" Rebecca asked, sensing they were about to get lost in the brambles again. She needed to stay focused on what mattered. Between sharing what she'd seen with her friends and her activities with Nigel, she didn't think she'd be able to sleep a wink that night anyhow.

Fortunately, Jo didn't hesitate before going on with, "He told the woman there would be no diamonds for her, she'd been a very bad girl, and he would give a diamond to someone else."

"Is he referring to the stolen diamond?" Caro asked.

"There isn't any other diamond worth mentioning that I know of," Rebecca said.

"Then Lord Lichfield is the thief," Jo said, practically hopping on the bed in excitement.

Rebecca shook her head. "Nigel thinks Lord Herrington did it."

"And I think the thief was Mr. Newman," Caro added.

"Who?" Rebecca and Jo asked in unison.

"Mr. Newman," Caro said. "He was wearing a mask with ram's horns."

"I saw him." Rebecca perked up. He had been awfully interested in the naked woman's jewels.

"I didn't," Jo sighed.

"I witnessed him—" she cleared her throat, "—engaged with one of the hired prostitutes."

"Were they hired, do you think?" Jo asked. "Not guests?"

Caro waved the question away. "Men have been hiring whores for parties exactly like that one for centuries, and that woman was certainly a whore. She looked bored to tears as Mr. Newman—" Again, she cleared her throat. "Regardless, they were in the same position as the other night, and as he—" Caro sighed. "It really is difficult relating this story without using the proper verbiage."

"Go on, then," Rebecca prompted her.

"As he tupped her," Caro continued, "he kept slipping her jewels off and pocketing them."

"Wait!" Rebecca jumped off the bed, arms outstretched. "Did you see his bum? Did you see the birthmark?"

Caro sighed and shook her head. "This time they were facing toward me. Which is how I could see how bored the woman was."

Rebecca sighed and sank to sit on her bed. "I have to find a way to tell Nigel all of this."

As it happened, she didn't have to worry about how to get in touch with Nigel. After a supremely sleepless night—for Jo and Caro too, if all the shifting and frustrated sighs that sounded through the night were any indication—she was treated to a hand-delivered note at breakfast.

"What is it?" Jo asked, leaning over her shoulder as she opened it.

Rebecca scanned the contents, swallowing an excited squeal. It was an invitation to spend the day with Verity, which could only mean one thing—it was actually an invitation to spend the day with Nigel.

Rebecca, Jo, and Caro darted looks down the table, to where Miss Dobson appeared to be falling asleep in her sausages at the head table—which made all three of them giggle for a variety of reasons. When Rebecca got up and sedately made her way to the head table to ask if she had permission to leave the school for the day, Miss Dobson merely shushed her, eyes still closed, and gestured for her to go away.

An hour later, Rebecca alighted from the Landsbury carriage—which had waited at the door for her—and rushed up the steps and into Landsbury House. Her heart nearly leapt out of her chest when she found Nigel waiting in the foyer for her.

"Nigel," she exclaimed, rushing to him, ready to leap into his arms. "I didn't expect you to send for me so soon."

Nigel caught her as she leapt the final few feet toward him, holding her close and spinning in a half circle so that her momentum didn't knock them both over. He kissed her, but his ardor melted into seriousness far too fast.

"After you left last night," he said in a rush, taking her hand and leading her right back out the door to the waiting carriage, "I trailed Herrington through the party."

"Did he confess to stealing the diamond?" she asked as he helped her back into the carriage. The driver seemed to know they would be leaving again the moment they arrived. "Only, Caro thinks—"

"No," Nigel cut her off with a frown. "But Herrington spent quite a bit of time speaking to Lichfield."

Rebecca blushed, wondering if that was before or after Lord Lichfield spanked the woman Jo had seen him with. But, of course, it would have been after, otherwise Jo wouldn't have witnessed the pseudo-punishment.

"Hyde Park Corner," Nigel told the driver once he and Rebecca were seated. As the carriage lurched into motion, he went on with, "The two of them arranged to meet in Hyde Park this morning."

"And we're going to intercept them?" Rebecca caught her breath at the rush of excitement that filled her.

"In a manner of speaking," Nigel said. "I had Lady Landsbury send for you so that I might have an excuse to be strolling through Hyde Park, so that I won't look suspicious if either Herrington or Lichfield spot me."

Rebecca grinned at him, resting her hand on his knee. "Is that truly the reason?"

Nigel's serious expression turned gruff, and he cleared his throat. He was shier in daylight than he was at night, in a secret passage. "That's what I told Gibbon, my superior," he said, a spark in his eyes.

Rebecca laughed deep in her throat. Part of her wanted to shift so that she straddled him, then and there, in the carriage. She wanted to finish what they'd started at Landsbury House earlier in the week. The motion of the carriage would be a great help. But another part of her longed to have his promise to her about a bed and privacy and time fulfilled. And yet another part of her wanted to catch the diamond thief.

"Do you still think Lord Herrington is the thief?" she asked, settling uncomfortably in her seat. She deserved a commendation from the king for her restraint.

"If not Herrington, then Lichfield," Nigel said.

"And Miss Dobson," Rebecca nearly shouted, forgetting what Caro thought about Mr. Newman and jumping half out of her seat. She turned to him, full of energy in a flash. "I have to tell you what we all saw last night."

The rest of the way to Hyde Park, Rebecca related the story of everything she, Caro, and Jo had seen in their various adventures through the secret passageways of the East India Company's house. Nigel seemed to share her distaste at everything having to do with Miss Dobson behaving badly, but he was interested in her comments about diamonds—both from Miss Dobson and Lord Lichfield.

"Miss Dobson wasn't in the house when the diamond went missing," Nigel said as they reached the park and alighted from the carriage. They kept their voices down as they strolled into the busy gardens. "But she could still be an accessory to the theft."

"I think so too," Rebecca agreed.

It was a pleasant, early-autumn day, and Hyde Park was crowded. Fine ladies and gentlemen with nothing better to do than take the air strolled along the park's many paths. Several nannies with small children or prams paraded through the gardens. A handful of working-class men and men who appeared to be clerks were enjoying their luncheon on the sloping greens around the Serpentine. There were vendors selling everything from tea to sweets to roasted nuts, and even a few performers in search of a day's wage for their entertainments. In short, it was the perfect place to see and be seen, or to blend in so as not to be seen at all.

"How will we find them?" Rebecca asked as Nigel escorted her along the north bank of the Serpentine. "Hyde Park is quite large."

"They'll stick to the shadows for their nefarious deeds," Nigel growled, seeming so sure of himself that Rebecca's insides grew warm.

"Then shouldn't we as well?" she asked.

He paused and studied her. Rebecca suddenly wished her one and only non-uniform gown had a lower neckline. Or that she wasn't wearing a gown at all. Although that would have been a bit beyond the pale in the middle of Hyde Park.

Nigel seemed to know where her thoughts were heading. "Perhaps if we found a suitable cluster of bushes in a spot the gentlemen in question would be likely to transact their business."

He started forward once more, picking up his pace and searching out a likely spot for spying. Or for other things. She noted a few close-growing stands of trees. There were even small structures at the extreme far end of the park, closer to Kensington Palace, although that did seem like an excessive distance to walk.

"What about over there?" Rebecca pointed to a cluster of bushes nearer the Serpentine.

Nigel stopped in his tracks. At first she thought it was because he agreed with her choice of concealing spots. A moment later, she realized he had spied something. She turned to look, only to see Lord Lichfield and Lord Herrington riding slowly and in close quarters along one of the outermost paths of the park.

"Damn," Nigel muttered.

Rebecca wasn't certain if his oath was because the two men were far away or because they were on horseback, or because they'd had the misfortune to find exactly what they were supposedly looking for when it would have been much nicer simply to conceal themselves out of sight and let nature take its course between them.

A moment later, they had an even greater problem.

"My word. Lady Rebecca Burgess, is that you?"

Rebecca gasped and whipped around in time to see Mrs. Philomena Hodges—Jo's mother—and Jo's married sister, Mrs. Wilma Everett, walking toward them.

"Damn," Nigel muttered again, still focused on Lord

Lichfield and Lord Herrington. "Herrington is handing something off to him."

"Whatever are you doing here?" Mrs. Hodges asked, a good deal of censure mingled with her look of surprise. "And who is this sturdy gentleman and why are you without a chaperone?"

Rebecca's jaw dropped, and she scrambled to find words—any words—to explain herself. Nigel noticed something was wrong and pivoted to frown at Mrs. Hodges and Mrs. Everett. "Who are you?" he asked, sounding more like the Runner he was than any sort of gentleman.

"Mr. Kent, this is Mrs. Hodges and Mrs. Everett," Rebecca rushed to introduce them. "My friend Josephine's mother and sister."

"Oh." Nigel moved into a surprisingly elegant bow a little too belatedly. "Forgive my manners, madam, madam." He nodded to each woman in turn.

"Why aren't you in school?" Mrs. Hodges asked without any attempt to engage Rebecca in polite conversation. "That school is supposed to keep a sharp eye and a firm grip on its pupils. Why else do you think we sent Josephine there?"

"Josephine," Mrs. Everett sighed and shook her head, as though Jo were a trial and a burden rather than one of the most delightful friends Rebecca had ever had.

"You should be at school," Mrs. Hodges repeated.

"Yes," Mrs. Everett agreed. "At school."

"Lady Rebecca is not a child," Nigel told the women, his eyes narrowed.

"It's not that kind of school," Mrs. Hodges snapped back, her jaw clenched.

"Mr. Kent is a Bow Street Runner," Rebecca blurted.

She instantly regretted her statement. Part of her hoped it would intimidate Jo's mother and sister and shut them up. Instead, they gaped at her as though she were the criminal Nigel had apprehended.

"What have you done now?" Mrs. Hodges asked in a voice full of dread. "You haven't corrupted my Josephine, have you?"

"I believe that job is already done, Mama," Mrs. Everett muttered.

Mrs. Hodges shushed her with a scowl, then turned that scowl on Nigel, as though demanding he answer her question.

Fortunately for Rebecca, Nigel thought faster than her.

"Lady Rebecca is helping me with an investigation," he said in a soft but dismissive tone. "So if you will excuse us."

He tugged on Rebecca's arm, escorting her away from the two imperious women without taking his leave of them.

"That was a bit rude," Rebecca whispered as they started back along the path toward Hyde Park Corner, the way Lord Lichfield and Lord Herrington had gone.

Then she giggled. "I rather enjoyed being rude to those two. From what Jo says, they make her life miserable."

Nigel's only response was to grunt. "It's never good to run into people you know during an investigation."

"It's never good to run into people like that, whether you know them or not," Rebecca said. She only wanted to forget the encounter. "Can you still see Lord Lichfield and Lord Herrington?" she asked.

Nigel grunted again. "They're about to leave the park."

"Oh, dear," Rebecca sighed. "Now I'm twice as vexed that we were waylaid by Jo's family. Can we catch up to them?"

"Perhaps," Nigel said. He glanced to her and his expression softened. "It's a long-shot, but perhaps there might be a way to ascertain where they are going."

"Ooh, how?" she asked, brightening again.

Nigel's expression widened into a smile, and he switched from cradling her hand in his elbow to holding her hand. "We follow them."

CHAPTER 7

*H*e'd gone completely mad. He was breaking every rule of the Runners and of common sense. Inviting Rebecca to be a part of his investigation of Herrington and Lichfield was a flimsy excuse at best to spend time with her. If Gibbon found out, he would likely sack Nigel on the spot. But he had been able to think of little else besides Rebecca for days—months, if he was honest with himself—and at the time, bringing her along with him as he worked had seemed like the best way to kill two birds with one stone.

He was an utter fool.

"There they go," Rebecca gasped, clinging tighter to his hand and pointing toward the gate at Hyde Park Corner. "They're leaving the park."

"I see them."

Nigel picked up his pace, hoping Rebecca could keep up. She surprised him by scurrying along at his side without any signs of flagging. Perhaps she was made of tougher stuff after all.

Of course, that thought did nothing at all to focus his thoughts on his prey. He glanced to Rebecca, studying her flushed cheeks and determined expression as best he could while dodging startled walkers on the path they jogged down. They were drawing far too much attention —for an investigation and for an unmarried man and woman alone together in public. If anyone recognized Rebecca, it was entirely likely her reputation would be ruined forever.

But she had already been recognized, and as for her reputation....

"Hurry, hurry," she urged him as they reached Hyde Park Corner. "They're turning a corner."

Nigel tugged her out of the path of a man on horse-back entering the park, slipping his arm around her waist. A trio of fashionable ladies gasped at his gesture and instantly started whispering behind their hands, their expressions disapproving. Nigel frowned at the reaction, but it wasn't enough for him to remove his arm from Rebecca's waist as they rushed around the corner to Park Lane.

"They've turned again," Rebecca said as they hurried on.

"I think I know where they're going," Nigel said with a grim smile. "And we're in luck."

"We are?" Rebecca glanced up at him as they turned onto a side street.

Nigel took her hand again once they were out of the main flow of traffic. The sounds of the main street and the park gave way to more enclosed, intimate noise. Nigel was certain he could even hear the clop of Herrington's and Lichfield's horses ahead.

They reached an intersection, and he gestured for Rebecca to stop. Carefully, he glanced around the corner and was rewarded by the sight of Herrington and Lichfield dismounting in front of a posh pub called The Silver Hart. Nigel grinned. The two couldn't have played into his hands more perfectly.

As soon as they'd disappeared inside the pub, he gestured for Rebecca to continue with him.

"We aren't going to a pub, are we?" she whispered. "I've always wanted to see the inside of a pub."

Her comment, combined with the certainty that he had the diamond thief cornered, made Nigel smile. "We aren't going to the pub," he said as he crossed the street and strode swiftly along the pavement to the building across from the pub. "We're going to watch them and nab them when they leave."

"Watch them?" Rebecca asked. "How? From where?"

He grinned at her, stepping up to the front door of the building across from the pub. "From my flat."

Rebecca's eyes went wide, as well they should. Nigel pushed open the door, escorting her inside a large hallway with a staircase leading up and several closed doors deeper into the hall. He took the stairs, rounding a landing and climbing to the second floor. Once there, he drew a key from the pocket of his waistcoat and unlocked a door that led to a modest flat with windows looking out the front of the building.

"This is where you live?" Rebecca asked, a touch of awe in her voice, as she walked into the main room and looked around.

Nigel dropped her hand and strode deeper into the room, tidying up the papers he'd left strewn about and the dishes from last night's supper. "It is," he said. "Well, it's where I reside at present. I have another residence in London that remains unoccupied at the moment."

He hoped she was too absorbed in studying his surroundings to ask questions. He was in luck.

"You live in a flat just off of Hyde Park," she said, walking to the window with a slight frown.

"I do," he said, taking his dishes to the small kitchen at the back of the flat before striding across the main room to stand behind her.

Rebecca peeked out the window, her fingertips resting on the glass. "Why, you can see Kensington Palace from here."

"On a clear day, yes," Nigel said.

She turned to him. Her eyes widened to find him standing so close to her, but she went on with, "This flat must cost a fortune."

He grinned at her, quickly losing the thread of the conversation. He could smell her fresh scent, feel the heat of her body. "It does," he admitted, raising a hand to trace his fingertips along her pink cheek.

Rebecca sucked in a breath that made her breasts rise against her bodice...which scattered Nigel's thoughts even more. Perhaps bringing her to his home wasn't a wise idea either.

She seemed to confirm that when she asked, "How can a Bow Street Runner afford a flat overlooking Hyde Park?"

"It doesn't really overlook the park," he said, slipping his other hand to her waist and pulling her close. "Those buildings block most of the view. The only reason I can see the palace is because I'm on a higher floor and there's a gap in the buildings across the street."

"But still," she went on. "It must be expensive to—"

He stopped her with a kiss. He lowered his hand to her backside and lifted her to the tips of her toes as his mouth slanted over hers. It was a reckless, mad thing to do, but he couldn't stop himself. Her questions would lead to answers he wasn't ready to give. But more than that, he couldn't think with her so close. So he kissed her, teasing her lips with his teeth and tongue before invading her mouth to suck on her sweetness.

She sighed with need, which only spurred him on. His cock jumped to hardness, straining against his breeches as if it had a mind and memory of its own. It had come so close to plumbing her depths just a few days ago, and now it wouldn't be denied. He gripped her backside possessively and ground against her hips. The movement shot bolts of pleasure through him even as it told her he wouldn't stop until they were both satisfied this time.

A peel of laughter sounded from the street below, loud enough to be heard through the closed window. As aroused as he was, Nigel's instincts as a Runner flashed to the forefront. He leaned back, breaking their kiss, and glanced out the window. Rebecca groaned in disappointment as he spotted Herrington and Lichfield striding out of the pub. The two wore smiles—though they glanced up and down the street as though afraid to be seen. They shook hands, said something that Nigel couldn't hear as the boy from the pub brought their horses up from the mews, then each mounted and went their separate ways.

Tension spiked in Nigel along with the urge to do something, to take action. He flinched away from the window, but before he could take so much as a single step, Rebecca moaned, "No!"

She grabbed the lapels of his jacket and stared pleadingly up at him. "No," she repeated. "We cannot be interrupted again. We will not be interrupted again. I demand that you ravish me."

Nigel's brow shot up. It wasn't the only thing that shot up. Blood pumped through him, and the urgency to follow and catch the thieves shifted to the pounding need to make Rebecca his, once and for all. And yet, the need that flashed through every part of him like an explosion was contradictory to everything he'd ever been taught.

"I want you, Nigel," Rebecca went on, her breath coming in short pants. "I want you to touch me all over. I want you to do what you did to me the other day at Verity's house. I want your manly weapon inside of me. I'll do anything you want me to do. I don't care if it makes me a harlot. I burn for you. I need to be bad, so very, very bad."

It was utter, ridiculous madness. Polite, respectable young ladies were not supposed to beg for sex. The sort of woman a man of substance should marry was not supposed to sigh and moan and offer her virginity as a plaything on an ordinary afternoon. Rebecca truly was behaving as a harlot—at least by every definition society gave to the word. But Nigel had never wanted to possess and use and pleasure a woman in every way more in his life. He wanted to marry Rebecca—not to prevent her from being a whore, but because that was precisely what she wanted to be. For him.

He surged into her, closing his arms around her and lowering his hands to her backside. He pivoted to push her into the wall beside the window, lifting her so that she straddled his waist as he pinned her to the wall. His mouth crashed over hers, plundering her willing sweetness. The sounds of pleasure and surrender that she made spurred him on, making him wonder already how fast he could recover after coming deep inside of her so that he could fuck her a second time.

Rebecca's sigh of relief as Nigel lifted her and trapped her against the wall so that he could ravish her quickly turned into a moan of desire. Her entire body felt

as though it were being consumed by fire. They were
upright, but Nigel was wedged between her legs, jerking
against her in a way that teased what else could happen
between them. All she wanted to do was spread her legs
wider, but she had to circle them around his waist to keep
from falling over. That didn't stop her skirts from getting
in the way, however.

She cried out in wordless protest, wanting nothing
more than to cast aside her clothes entirely so that her
skin could slide against Nigel's. Her cry was swallowed
by his mouth and his tongue plundering her. His
aggression sent tingles of delicious fright through her.
He was so strong, so large, that he could do anything to
her. She hoped he would do anything and everything
to her.

Too soon, he stepped back, breaking their kiss so that
he could catch his breath. Rebecca slid to stand, wobbling
slightly.

"I promised you a bed," he growled, fire in his eyes.

At that moment, she would have been perfectly
happy with the floor, but he took her hand and led her
across the main room and through a half-opened door
into his bedroom. The room was untidy without being a
complete mess. His bed wasn't made, though the covers
had been thrown haphazardly over it. Rebecca didn't
care. It was a bed, and it was his.

"I have to get out of my clothes," she said in a near
panic, twisting her arms behind her to grab at the ties
holding her gown closed.

"Let me help you with that," he growled, stepping behind her and making quick work of the ties.

Rebecca wriggled and gasped, pulling at the muslin of her gown as though it were laced with spiders, as soon as the ties were undone. Nigel went to work shedding his own clothes as she peeled away her layers, cursing every one.

"Clothing is such an irritating nuisance," she panted as she pushed her gown over her hips.

"It's a waste of time," Nigel agreed, unbuttoning his waistcoat and throwing it on the floor.

Rebecca giggled as their efforts to undress turned into a sort of race. She kicked her gown and petticoats aside, fumbling with the closures of her stays in an effort to beat him to nakedness. He was just tugging off his boots, balancing first on one leg, then the other, as he did so, by the time she pulled her chemise up over her head, leaving her completely exposed to him.

Nigel froze as his second boot hit the floor, staring at her with wide, wolfish eyes. He straightened. He still wore his breeches, but they were glaringly tented. "I've wanted to see your tits again more than you can know," he said, his voice low and filled with hunger.

Rebecca glanced down at her breasts then back to him, thrusting her chest forward. Her nipples were well on their way to being tight points, and her breasts felt heavier than usual and desperate to be touched. "Here they are," she said breathlessly.

He took a large step toward her, kicking aside their

clothes as he did. His large hands closed around her breasts with such possessiveness that Rebecca gasped. The sound turned into a groan as he squeezed and rubbed his thumbs over her nipples. The pleasure his simple attentions gave her shot straight to her core, making her feel as though liquid heat were filling her sex.

Nigel didn't stop there. He bent his knees enough to lower his mouth to her breasts, drawing one nipple fully into his mouth. There was no teasing or coaxing, he simply took what he wanted, nipping her with his teeth and stroking her with his tongue. Rebecca gasped and shivered...and had no idea what to do with her hands. Her body pulsed with pleasure that was so potent she felt as though she might come apart then and there.

The moment she realized she could thread her hands through his thick, dark hair, he sank to his knees. His mouth broke away from her breast and trailed across her belly and lower. He nudged her knees apart, and she widened her stance just in time for him to bury his face in the curls between her legs.

"Nigel," she gasped, her eyes going wide, then heavy-lidded as his tongue flickered out to pleasure her. She gripped tight handfuls of his hair, hardly believing he could make her feel that way when she was standing up. Who had ever heard of such a thing?

Apparently, Nigel had. He pleasured her with her lips and tongue in a way that sent need coursing through her without being quite intense enough to send her splashing over the edge. At least, at first. When he stroked a hand up her inner thigh and plunged his fingers deep into her wet, aching core, the combination of pleasure sent her careening over the edge.

She cried out as her body throbbed with orgasm. He made a sound of victorious pleasure and continued to lick and stroke her until her tremors slowed. The whole thing was so overwhelming that Rebecca's legs gave out. Nigel seemed to sense what she was feeling and managed to lower her to his bed before she fell.

As soon as she lay there, her legs sprawled over the edge of the bed as she lay on her back, he stood and reached for the falls of his breeches. Rebecca lifted herself to her elbows to watch as he undid them and stripped them off, kicking them aside. Then he stood in front of her completely naked. The large, firm muscles of his torso, arms, and legs, showed how powerful he really was, but it was his long, thick cock that had her full attention. He was so large that her thighs shuddered and her sex squeezed with both fright and need at the sight of him. His tip was wide and flared and already slick with moisture. He stood straight up, like the Ancient Greek depictions of satyrs that she'd seen. And there she was, naked, splayed, and wet on his bed, completely at his mercy. Nothing had ever been so arousing.

She sat straight, reaching for him. "I want to touch it," she said, surprised at how dusky her voice sounded. "I want to taste it."

He pushed her hands aside and advanced on her, tipping her back until she lay open to him once more.

"No," he said in a choked voice. "I'm already too close. I want to come inside of you, not in your hands or your mouth." He bent over her, tugging her hips toward him while his feet remained on the ground. "There will be time for all that later," he said bringing his hips into contact with hers and rubbing the underside of his penis against her already enflamed sex. "But once we get there," he went on in a gravely whisper, "I want you to swallow my cock so deep that it fills every inch of you."

His words shouldn't have been so arousing, but the image of submission that popped to Rebecca's mind— thanks to what she'd already witnessed her sister doing— was wildly erotic instead of mildly humiliating. She wanted to pleasure Nigel that way, to see his face contorted with arousal, but not just then. Just then she wanted—

"Oh, yes," she gasped as Nigel completed her thoughts with actions.

He guided his impossibly large cock to her entrance, pushing in slowly, but only until her body resisted. When he stopped, she held her breath and squeezed her eyes shut. But instead of breeching her maidenhood, he pulled out, then teased her by pushing in by an inch once more. A spike of frustration joined the mad desire that pulsed through her, and she lifted herself to her elbows again so she could watch his actions. Desire and strained control pinched his face.

"Please, Nigel," she gasped, her eyes trained on his

thick length as he stood poised between her widely-spread legs. "Take me."

"I'll hurt you," he said, his voice strained.

"Yes," she said, meeting his eyes. "And I'll like it, I swear."

That seemed to decide him. He leaned all the way over her, jerking into her with a firm, fast stroke.

Rebecca gasped. It did hurt. Like he had split her in two. But he was the one who had hurt her, and she loved him. The pain didn't matter, because deep, deep pleasure followed quickly behind it. "Oh!" she sighed, straining into his invasion.

When he let out a growling breath and began to move, it was all worth it. She was certain he was being deliberately careful at first, thrusting slowly. He kissed her as well, not the punishing, passionate kisses from before, but sweet, almost apologetic kisses that came straight from his heart. He slipped a hand under the small of her back, lifting her so that he could plunder her more deeply as the speed and power of his thrusts grew.

It was heavenly. Rebecca sighed and gasped and made other sounds she didn't have words for in time to his thrusts. It was so good tears sprung to her eyes. She was his, and it was every bit as wonderful as she'd always imagined it would be.

He stretched and claimed her, his thickness stroking her inside and bringing her right back to the edge of climax. It was pure bliss to have him use her for his own pleasure, and when the sounds coming from him turned loud and primal as he neared his completion, she burst into another throbbing wave of orgasm that had her crying out in victory.

His cry joined hers a moment later, and a rush of warmth filled her as his body tensed, his final thrust claimed her, and his body gradually slowed and softened. He stayed as firmly inside of her as his penis softened, and they both simply lay there, entwined and panting.

At last, when she felt enough of her strength return, Rebecca wriggled under him until she embraced him with her arms and legs. "How long until we can do that again?" she said.

Nigel chuckled. The vibrations shivered through her, and she squeezed her inner muscles around his soft length. In the end, though, he pulled out of her. But only so that he could reposition them more comfortably and fully in the bed.

"I need a few minutes," he said in a sleepy voice.

"Not too long, I hope." She grinned, snuggling against him.

"Not too long," he repeated. He rolled to his side with their heads resting on his pillow. He molded her body against his, lifting her leg over his waist. "First a nap."

"Agreed," she sighed, draping her arm over his muscular side.

"Then I'm going to play with your titties for a while," he said, his voice still hazy, a lazy smile spreading across his lips. "Then I'm going to flip you to your stomach and tease you into thinking I'm going to fuck you in the ass."

"You're not?" she asked, raising an eyebrow, knowing he was teasing her without knowing the extent of the joke.

"Not today," he chuckled. "You're not ready. I'm going to make you think I will, but then I'll just take you in the pussy from behind until you come hard on my cock."

Rebecca sighed and snuggled up to him as though he'd described a summer's picnic in the country. "That sounds lovely."

"And then, if there's time before supper, I want you on top so I can thrust balls-deep and put babies right in your womb."

"Very well," Rebecca sighed, her eyes closing. "But then you must marry me."

"There's no question of that," he said, just as sleepy as she was. "If you still want me once you know."

Rebecca merely hummed as sleep overtook her, although at the back of her mind, a voice whispered, "Know what?"

CHAPTER 8

There simply wasn't time for Nigel to fulfill all his naughty promises to Rebecca before the hour grew short and she had to return to the school. He did, however, roll her onto her back after their short nap, spread her legs, and plunder her raw a second time. Rebecca was certain she looked ridiculous with her legs splayed wide to her sides and her face contorted in ecstasy as he thrust his massive manhood into her over and over, faster and faster, until she was genuinely worried that it would be too much for her inexperienced body. She loved every moment of his punishing ardor, though, and came apart with a cry of release only a few moments before he groaned with completion.

Of course, an hour or so later, as she stepped gingerly down from the carriage he'd borrowed from Lord Landsbury to return her to the school, she wasn't sure their activity had been wise. She simply couldn't manage to walk normally as she climbed the stairs to the school's front door and knocked for admittance.

She wasn't more than half a dozen steps into the school's front hall when Miss Dobson charged out of her office, her face like a thundercloud as she glared at Rebecca.

"Where have you been?" she demanded, marching so close that Rebecca stumbled a few, painful steps back.

Unfortunately, she winced as she stumbled. "I was visiting the Marchioness of Landsbury," she said, attempting to dazzle Miss Dobson with Verity's rank.

Miss Dobson continued to pursue her. She towered over Rebecca as she inched toward the wall. And then she sniffed. Her wrinkled face twisted into a triumphant grin. Rebecca gulped, wishing she'd thought to bathe after spending the afternoon in Nigel's bed.

"You smell like a whore," Miss Dobson said in a low, accusatory growl. "You smell like a dirty, filthy whore who has spent the day with her legs parted."

Rebecca opened her mouth to defend herself, but she had no defense. Miss Dobson was right, in a manner of speaking.

A flicker of movement on the stairs behind Miss Dobson caught Rebecca's eye. Jo and Caro froze in the middle of rushing down the stairs. Their jubilant expressions at the sight of Rebecca flashed to horror at the way Miss Dobson had her cornered.

"You've been rutting like a pig, haven't you?" Miss Dobson asked, raising her voice. A few of her pupils peeked around the corners from classrooms and the dining room. "You were entrusted to my care so that I could reform your disgraced morals, but you've thrown that back in my face by fucking every man that catches your fancy."

The watching pupils gasped at Miss Dobson's vulgar language, though a few directed their shock at Rebecca. Rebecca did the only thing she could think to do in order to save face.

"No, I didn't," she lied. At least, she hadn't gone to bed with every man, just one.

Without warning, Miss Dobson slapped her across the face. "Don't lie to me, you wicked harlot."

More gasps echoed around them. Jo and Caro rushed down the stairs as though they would come to Rebecca's rescue, but Miss Cade and Miss Warren, Miss Dobson's favorites students, blocked their way.

"Bad girls like you are punished," Miss Dobson went on. "Bad girls like you deserve everything they get."

She grabbed Rebecca's arm and dragged her down the hall to the narrow staircase that led down to the below-ground floors. At first, Rebecca thought Miss Dobson would drag her into the kitchen or the scullery to make her scrub pots or help the kitchen staff. Instead, she yanked her along the hall to a small door in an abandoned part of the downstairs hall.

Miss Dobson paused to fish a key from the ring attached to her belt and to open the door. Rebecca gulped in dread when the door creaked open into what looked like an unused wine cellar. It was dark and dank, but when Miss Dobson called, one of the kitchen maids brought a lamp. A bit of light did nothing to improve the look of the place. Empty, rotting wine racks lined the walls, and a few large, tapped barrels stood in the center of the room.

Miss Dobson pushed her toward one of the barrels, and when Rebecca knocked against it, she shoved her forward until she bent double, dangling helplessly over the barrel. Rebecca was too shocked to right herself and scramble away, and within a few seconds, it was too late.

"Bad girls will be punished accordingly," Miss Dobson said as she grabbed one of Rebecca's wrists and clamped shackles around it. "I will not have bad girls at my school." She clamped shackles around Rebecca's other wrist, then dashed around to do the same with her ankles.

A slither of fear rippled through Rebecca as she realized she was trapped over the barrel, unable to move her arms or legs, which were spread apart in a worrying way. Her fear became full-blown when Miss Dobson jerked her skirts up and over her head, exposing her bare bottom and worse, her sore sex.

"I knew it," Miss Dobson growled, presumably studying the evidence of the afternoon's activities.

Rebecca burst into tears. It was an unspeakable violation to be seen that way. What she and Nigel had done was for the two of them alone. It was wrong—so wrong—for anyone else to have a part in it, no matter how small.

But that thought brought with it memories of all the times she'd spied on her sister Mary with Lord Grey. It filled her with guilt at her own indiscretions and invasions. Even what she'd seen the diamond thief doing several days before. Those things were not meant for public display, they were for the participants alone. She felt more wretched than she would ever have imagined feeling.

Almost enough to agree when Miss Dobson repeated, "Wicked, bad, whores should be punished." Something scraped at the edge of the room.

A moment later, Rebecca gasped in shock and pain as Miss Dobson smacked her bare bottom hard with what must have been a paddle of some sort.

"Bad," Miss Dobson shouted, smacking her again. "Bad." Another vicious smack. "Bad!"

Rebecca cried out with each beating, not sure which was worse, the pain or the humiliation. But there was nothing she could do but scream out in protest and pray for a miracle.

NIGEL LEANED BACK IN HIS CHAIR NEAR THE FRONT of The Silver Hart pub, unable to wipe the smile off his face. Rebecca had been superb that afternoon. It had been worth every interruption and every false start to finally bed her. She'd surprised him with her eagerness and enjoyment of what would have frightened most women of her age and lack of experience. He wasn't

exactly small and elegant. Every part of him—*every* part
—was large and intimidating. That's what made him such
a perfect Runner, in spite of his birth and upbringing.

"Another whiskey?" Robbie, the pub's owner, asked
as he passed Nigel's table on his rounds.

Nigel shook his head and held up a hand. He was
technically there for work, after all. He'd reported in to
the Bow Street office after seeing Rebecca home to the
school and had discovered that his initial hunch about
The Silver Hart as the site of activity surrounding the
diamond had been right. A tip had come in that the thief
had arranged to meet a potential buyer at the pub. Nigel
was convinced Herrington and Lichfield had already
done the deal—and that he'd missed it while occupied
with Rebecca. He wasn't about to confess that to Gibbon,
even though he should. And Gibbon had been adamant
that the potential sale would take place that night instead
of in the afternoon. So there Nigel was, waiting for any
sign of Herrington or Lichfield's return. The two must
have set something up at the pub that afternoon in prepa-
ration for the meeting.

That afternoon. Nigel let out another contented
breath, indulging in his recent memories. He was certain
he looked like a bloody fool, sitting there, alone, a satisfied
grin on his face. But how could he help himself? The
image of Rebecca's sweet face as she came, the way her
eyes had glazed over with pleasure as she'd taken him—all
of him—into her tight, wet pussy had his cock hardening.
Nigel wasn't sure he'd ever been with a woman who had

wanted it as desperately as Rebecca had. He would never forget her plaintive cries as his thick length disappeared into her hungry quim. He'd been so turned on by the sight of their bodies joining that he'd almost missed watching her face when she came.

The pub felt entirely too hot, and Nigel was tempted to lean over and open the window beside him. Everything he'd been told since he was a boy said that he should abhor any woman who gave in to a man so freely or who enjoyed being fucked so soundly. He should write Rebecca off as a woman of shamelessly loose morals and cast her aside as an entertainment and nothing more. Men of his background were supposed to marry shy and retiring virgins who wept at the thought of being bedded, and who were only bedded by their husbands. But the way Rebecca had moaned with pleasure, the way she'd wanted to swallow him right off the bat, and the way she begged for more once he was in her had his heart in shreds. He didn't just want her, knowing she had the soul of a harlot, he loved her. He loved her so much that he would seek out a special license at first light tomorrow. He'd marry her as soon as possible, get her out of that ridiculous school, and bed her using every position he could think of, and a few he'd make up as they went along.

Those thoughts were so engaging that Nigel was on the verge of heading back to his flat so that he could choke his cock while thinking about her when a man wearing a cloak, his hat pulled down low enough to conceal his face, walked into the pub. Nigel sat straighter, his senses prickling. A dozen men and more had walked into the pub while he'd been sitting there, but he knew, he just knew, that the man in the cloak was connected to the diamond. It was in the hunch of his shoulders, the way he skulked straight into the darkest corner of the room without ordering a drink and sat, his face still hidden.

Nigel's heart pounded, thoughts of Rebecca temporarily forgotten. This was it. Tonight, he would catch the thief. He would make Herrington or Lichfield or whoever it was pay.

He was halfway out of his chair, mind spinning with ways to get close enough to the thief to overhear whatever conversations he was about to have, when the pub door slammed open again. This time, a woman dashed in, her eyes wide, her auburn hair in disarray. Several of the men sitting closest to the door cheered and brightened, raising glasses to her as though she were an actress entering the stage for the sole purpose of entertaining them.

Nigel frowned. He recognized the woman. She was one of Rebecca's friends. She'd been standing with her in the fenced garden the day of the theft. The woman glanced anxiously around, and as soon as her eyes settled on Nigel, she recognized him and looked as though she would weep in relief.

"Mr. Kent," she gasped, dodging around the tables to reach him. "Mr. Kent, thank God I've found you. Lord Landsbury said you'd be here."

Sure enough, Landsbury strode into the pub a moment later, his face etched with deep concern. He spotted Nigel instantly and made his way over.

"What's going on?" Nigel asked him.

It was the young woman who answered with, "Miss Dobson has taken Rebecca prisoner."

The bottom fell out of Nigel's stomach. His eyes went wide as he glanced to Landsbury.

"I know nothing about it," Landsbury said. "Miss Hodges came to me not twenty minutes ago, demanding we find you at once. All I know is that Lady Rebecca is in trouble."

"What kind of trouble?" Nigel asked. He glanced furtively to the corner where the thief was still waiting for whoever had plans to meet with him.

"She came back to the school this afternoon," the young woman—the pieces clicked into place, and Nigel realized she was Miss Josephine Hodges—said, grasping his arm. Her face went pink. "Miss Dobson knew exactly what she'd been doing. She dragged Rebecca down to the basement and—" Miss Hodges swallowed hard, looking sick. "None of us saw anything, but we could hear Rebecca screaming. Pearl, the kitchen maid, says that Miss Dobson beat her with a bread peel."

Rage pulsed through Nigel. He started toward the pub door, murder on his mind. Anyone who dared to lay a finger on Rebecca would have to answer to him, even if she was a woman. He would make Miss Dobson wish she'd never been born. He'd bring her school down around her ears if he had to.

"I snuck out through the secret passage," Miss Hodges went on as they made their way toward the door. "It has an exit into the mews. I knew I had to find you, that you could help."

As soon as he reached the door, Nigel paused. A second gentleman in a cloak, his face concealed, entered the pub. Expensive, Hessian boots peeked out from the hem of his cloak, and though his head was completely covered, Nigel could have sworn he saw bits of ginger hair poking out from under the brim. It was Herrington, he was certain, and he headed slowly but deliberately back through the pub toward the thief's table.

Frustration like nothing Nigel had ever known prickled through him. It was so intense that he clenched his jaw. There, in the back corner of The Silver Hart, the diamond could be changing hands. The cloaked men were clearly up to no good. His orders and his duty as a Runner were to apprehend criminals and bring the diamond thief to justice. But Rebecca needed him. She was trapped in an untenable position, helpless at the hands of a cruel and heartless woman. She needed him.

It tore him in two, but there was no dodging the truth of where he needed to be. Diamonds were things. They could wait. Rebecca was his heart, his life, his love, and his first priority in all things.

"Let's go," he growled to Landsbury and Miss Hodges. "How fast can we get to that damned school?"

CHAPTER 9

*N*igel couldn't move fast enough. As soon as he shot out of The Silver Hart, Lansbury and Miss Hodges behind him, he charged down the street with every intention of running all the way to Miss Dobson's School.

But Landsbury called after him, "Kent, where are you going, man? The carriage is right here."

Nigel pulled up short and spun around in time to see Landsbury handing Miss Hodges into a black lacquered carriage. Everything about it screamed "slow" in Nigel's mind, but he rushed back with a growl, jumping in after Miss Hodges.

Fortunately for him, Lord Lansbury was willing to overlook his rudeness as he told the driver, "Miss Dobson's Finishing School, Manchester Square, Marylebone," before climbing in behind Nigel.

Nigel gritted his teeth and tapped his foot against the

carriage wall as they headed north to Oxford Street. The traffic was abominable, as usual, and even once Landsbury's driver was able to cut through and take them up Duke Street, time felt as though it were wasting away. When they were blocked from proceeding into the square where the school stood, he pushed open the door with a frustrated growl.

As soon as his feet hit the pavement, he ran. But only a few yards into the square he slammed straight into a man heading in the other direction. Both of them grunted with the impact, and while Nigel barely managed to stay on his feet, the other man tumbled to the ground.

"Sorry," Nigel grumbled, extending an impatient hand. The least he could do before rushing to Rebecca's rescue was to help the man up.

"It was my fault. I failed to watch where I was going," the gentleman said.

As soon as he was fully on his feet, Nigel's eyes went wide. Staring back at him were the green eyes of Lord Rufus Herrington. His ginger hair was in disarray after taking a spill, but there was no mistaking the man. Lord Herrington. Suspected diamond thief. Standing right in front of him. Which meant he wasn't one of the two suspected thieves currently at The Silver Hart. And that meant that there was a distinct possibility he'd been wrong about the thief's identity.

But there wasn't time to investigate further.

"Excuse me, my lord," he murmured, rushing past

Herrington and around the corner to the front steps of the school.

He barely paused to bang on the door. As he pounded with one hand, he turned the handle with the other. Mercifully, the door was unlocked and he pushed it open before the startled maid he found on the other side could let him in.

"Where is she?" he demanded. "Take me to her at once."

Instead of following his order, the maid burst into tears and ran into the room just to the side of the front hall. It was just his luck that that room—a dining room, by the look of it—was filled with young ladies. Instantly, a ripple of interest passed through the room, benches were pushed back, and a throng of wide-eyed, awed young misses scampered to the doorway, presumably to get a look at him.

"He's so tall," one of them said.

"And so muscular," another added.

"And handsome," yet another said.

The ladies who had reached the doorway first were pushed aside by the next wave of hungry-looking ladies.

"I haven't seen a man up close in months," someone lamented from the side of the crush at the door.

"Does he smell manly?" someone else asked. "I'm certain he smells manly."

For a moment, Nigel was certain he'd lost his mind as a dozen or so young women sniffed in unison, then let out sighs of pleasure. The collective sound made the hair on the back of his neck stand up.

"What can we do for you, sir?" a young woman with dark hair and almond-shaped eyes wedged her way between the other ladies, grabbing his forearm. She let out a gasp of, "Oh, my," as though he'd made a welcomed advance on her.

"Stop being so forward, Felicity." Another of the ladies —a blonde with an alarmingly shapely figure—jostled her way out of the crowd and grabbed his other arm, stroking it and making eyes at him. "This man is our guest."

"I saw him first, Eliza," Felicity said.

"We both saw him at the same time," Eliza insisted.

"We could share," Felicity suggested with an impish look.

More than just the hair on the back of Nigel's neck began to stand up at the amorous attentions of the two young women. If he were a different sort of man entirely.... But no, he had a desperate mission in front of him.

"Where is Miss Dobson?" he asked, certain he looked like a thundercloud. "And where is Rebecca?"

As he spoke, Miss Hodges and Landsbury rushed through the door.

"She's this way," Miss Hodges said without pausing, gesturing for Nigel to follow.

Nigel broke away from his admirers and stormed down the hall at Miss Hodges' side. She appeared to be heading for a small staircase that led down, but before they could reach it, a voice shouted at them from an office at the end of the hall, "What is the meaning of this?"

Nigel changed directions so fast he nearly lost his balance. He recognized the voice all too well—Miss Dobson herself. As Miss Hodges started down the stairs, he marched into the vile woman's office.

"Where is Rebecca Burgess, you unforgivable cunt?" he demanded.

A split-second later, Nigel took in the room. It was ridiculously flowery for an office. One wall had a mostly-empty bookshelf. A fire was blazing in the grate. A single window was covered by curtains of a hideous salmon pink. A large desk took up the center of the room, a variety of switches resting on its top. But what snagged his attention closest of all was a second bookshelf behind the desk. A bookshelf that was angled about a foot and a half away from the wall...which appeared to be opened a crack.

As quickly as he spotted the secret passageway, he shunted it aside and advanced on Miss Dobson. "What have you done with Lady Rebecca?" he growled.

Miss Dobson's sour face tensed with shock. "Lady Rebecca? I don't know what you're talking about," she said, utterly unconvincingly. She backpedaled all the way to her desk, a hand clutching her heart, or at least the empty space where a heart should have been.

"I have it on good authority that you have illegally imprisoned Lady Rebecca and abused her," he growled, towering over Miss Dobson. It took every ounce of restraint he had not to raise a hand to the woman. He abhorred violence of all kinds directed against women, but at the moment, Miss Dobson was testing his patience sorely.

"L-Lady Rebecca disobeyed the rules of the school," Miss Dobson stammered, leaning backwards over her desk. "She obtained false permission to leave the school, lied about her whereabouts, and returned late." The woman blinked, then straightened with a scowl. "She was with you," she said.

Nigel ignored the accusation. He would gladly admit that Rebecca had been with him, and by the time he was finished, she would be with him always. He wouldn't let her stay another night under the wretched woman's roof.

"Where is she?" he growled as if he had a hardened killer cornered instead of a pernicious schoolteacher.

Miss Dobson swallowed and whimpered. "I own this school, sir," she squeaked. "The parents of these young women sign their daughters over into my care with an explicit understanding that I may use any means within my power to rid them of their scandalous and unacceptable proclivities. Contracts are signed granting permission to use corporal punishment if necessary. I have not done anything that that wicked young woman's parents have not already agreed to, nor that they would find fault in me doing."

Bile rose to the back of Nigel's throat, not because he thought she was lying, but because he knew she wasn't. He'd interviewed the right honorable Mr. and Mrs.

Burgess when Lord Grey was arrested for treason. They were as rotten as Grey and twice as corrupt. They were exactly the sort of people who would condone violence against their offspring as a way to bring them in line. It was a wonder Rebecca had turned out as soft and wonderful as she was. And it was about time he rescued her from the nightmare of her life.

"Where is she?" he repeated, balling his fists.

"She's downstairs," Miss Hodges called out from the doorway.

Nigel backed away from Miss Dobson and turned to her. The courageous young woman must have listened to the entire conversation. She gasped and darted out of sight as soon as Miss Dobson shifted her focus and scowled at the sight of her. The reaction was enough to prompt him to say, "If you hurt another one of the young ladies in your care, I will hurt you," before racing after her.

"She's in the old wine cellar," Miss Hodges said, breathless and miserable, when Nigel marched back into the hall. Rebecca's other friend, the blonde one, had joined her, and the two clasped hands, like sisters sentenced to the guillotine. "Hurry," Miss Hodges said.

Nigel didn't need to be told twice. He charged down the stairs, ready to do whatever it took to free Rebecca.

EVERY PART OF REBECCA HURT. HER STOMACH HURT from the barrel she was strung over digging into her for what felt like hours. Her wrists and ankles hurt where the shackles Miss Dobson had locked around them chafed. Her head pounded from being pointed downward for so long. Her backside throbbed in stinging agony from the blows Miss Dobson had landed. And if she were honest, her feminine parts were still sore from everything she'd done with Nigel.

But most of all, her pride was severely wounded. Miss Dobson had left her in the pitch-black cellar with her skirts tossed up over her head and her stinging bottom exposed. Even worse than that, her posterior faced the door—a door that had opened at least half a dozen times while she'd been trapped over the barrel. She had no idea who had peeked in to see her that way, but whoever they were, they had laughed and whispered before slamming the door shut on her and laughing some more. She would have bet a gold guinea it was Miss Cade, Miss Conyer, and Miss Warren, Miss Dobson's pets, but she had no way to prove it.

The humiliation was acute, and Rebecca's spirits had dropped to a pitiful low when thumping from the floor above her shook her out of the stupor she'd fallen into. She was only able to raise her head a little, but when she turned one ear to the ceiling, the sounds of a commotion were clear. Hope began to peek through the darkness in her heart. Something was happening. She squeezed her eyes shut, praying that whatever it was, it would mean the end of her torment. She wouldn't have minded the end of Miss Dobson either.

Sure enough, within minutes, the commotion grew louder, switching from the floor above her to the hallway outside the cellar where she was imprisoned. She held her breath as a masculine shout sounded through the door. She couldn't hear the words, but she would have known Nigel's voice anywhere.

"Nigel," she cried out with as much force as she could manage. She pulled at the shackles on her wrists, but instantly stopped when her efforts caused nothing but pain.

A moment later, the cellar door banged open and light spilled into the room.

"My God," Nigel shouted in shock.

Rebecca could only imagine what he thought of the site of her, bound and exposed as she was. "Nigel," she called to him, beyond caring how pitiful she felt.

She couldn't see him in her position, but she felt him march across the room in a few, thudding strides. He lifted her skirts, covering her fully and sending a surprise jolt of pain across the sensitive skin of her backside.

"I'll have your head for this," he growled to who Rebecca could only assume was Miss Dobson. "Release her from these barbaric chains at once."

"I haven't done anything wrong," Miss Dobson's voice echoed through the room along with the sound of keys jangling. "I told you, every punishment at this school has been explicitly described to the parents of my charges and approved of."

A sick knot formed in Rebecca's stomach, even as the

shackles around first her ankles, then her wrists loosened and dropped away. She shouldn't have been surprised. Hadn't her father gone on at length about how young women should have the wickedness beaten out of them on several occasions? And her mother had spoken repeatedly about the necessity of nipping pride in the bud.

"This is an atrocity," another male voice said. "The law will hear about this."

Rebecca had the horrible feeling the voice belonged to Lord Landsbury and that he'd seen her before Nigel had covered her.

"I've done nothing illegal, I swear it," Miss Dobson insisted, though she sounded more than a little mad.

Rebecca tried to move, tried to push herself up and away from the barrel, but she was too weak and in too much pain. Her efforts only lasted a moment before Nigel lifted her, cradling her in his powerful arms.

"My darling," he said, more emotion in his voice than she thought was possible for a man. "I'm so sorry. I'll never let anything like this happen to you again."

In spite of everything, Rebecca's eyes went wide. "You had nothing to do with this. It was her doing, not yours."

"You ungrateful harlot," Miss Dobson yelped. "It's my reputation you've put on the line with your whoring. Mine and my school's."

Nigel's arms and torso went rock-hard with fury around Rebecca. He marched forward. At first she thought he would attack Miss Dobson—who turned with a shriek and dashed into the hall—but he merely carried her into the light.

"If your reputation suffers, it is your own fault, madam," he growled. "Don't think I haven't seen you cavorting next door when Khan hosts his entertainments."

Miss Dobson gasped in offense, but her face went pink and her eyes wide. "I never!"

"You did just last week," Rebecca managed to say with a fair amount of force in her accusation. "I saw you drunk and exposing yourself, pleasuring two men at once." That had, in fact, been what Jo witnessed, but that didn't make it less true.

Miss Dobson's eyes popped even wider. "That was you?" she gasped. She stopped at the bottom of the stairs, preventing Nigel from carrying her up to the ground floor, where Rebecca could already see several of her fellow pupils gathered, eager to watch the unfolding drama. "I knew that was you," Miss Dobson went on, her tone turning accusatory. "You are a whore. A filthy little —" She stopped short when Lord Lansbury advanced toward her and scrambled up the stairs. "But how did you know about—" She stopped again as Nigel marched up the stairs after her, forcing her into the throng of her students. It was either confess what Jo had seen to every eager pair or ears or keep her mouth shut.

"I'm taking Miss Hodges out of here," Nigel declared when they reached the top of the stairs.

"But you can't," Miss Dobson said as he barged past

her, carrying Rebecca straight for the door. "Her parents pay me to keep her here."

Rebecca caught sight of Jo and Caro watching the unfolding scene from the staircase leading to the first floor. Their eyes were full of tears, though Rebecca couldn't tell if they were happy or miserable tears.

"The Hodges are abroad," Nigel said, marching for the door. "And I doubt they will ever return to England. I'll have words for them if they do."

The excited, murmuring young ladies of the school jumped out of Nigel's way as he pushed on. Lord Landsbury rushed ahead, opening the door for them when they reached it.

"But where will you take her?" Miss Dobson skittered along after them, shoving any girl unfortunate enough to get in her way. "You can't just pluck a young woman out of a respectable school."

"There is nothing respectable about this school," Nigel said as he reached the door and turned to face her. "I am opening an investigation into your conduct and practices in the morning."

"You can't—"

"Expect the Runners in the morning."

"Runners?" one of the young ladies asked.

"Bow Street Runners? Here?" another followed.

Within seconds, excited ripples spread through the hall and the adjoining rooms.

"Remind me to tell Gibbon only to send the most stalwart, unimpeachable Runners we have to the school,"

Nigel muttered to Rebecca. "Ones that preferred men would be best.

Of all things, Rebecca snorted with laughter. Nigel turned to carry her out to the street and hopefully to the carriage she could see waiting in the dark beyond the sidewalk.

"You cannot steal a woman from my school," Miss Dobson insisted, rushing after them. "It's abduction."

"I'm not stealing her," Nigel called over his shoulder as he lowered Rebecca carefully to her feet by the side of the carriage. Lord Landsbury held the door open for her. "I'm marrying her."

Rebecca's jaw dropped. Nigel turned away from Miss Dobson and the school and grinned at her. In spite of the pain that still lashed her, Rebecca had never been happier.

CHAPTER 10

*R*ebecca's happiness instantly dented as she climbed into Lord Landsbury's carriage and attempted to sit.

"Oh," she moaned, balancing her sore backside and body on her hands so that she didn't have to lower it all the way to the seat. Even cushioned, the seats weren't soft enough after what she'd suffered.

Nigel instantly sensed her predicament when he stepped up into the carriage. With a dark scowl, he sat on the seat with Rebecca, then lifted her into his arms. He positioned her carefully so that her backside rested in the space between his knees with little direct contact to anything and his powerful arms held her there. She only winced slightly when Lord Landsbury jostled the carriage as he stepped inside.

"If I had had any idea how wicked that Miss Dobson

woman was," Lord Landsbury began in a growl, "I would have done whatever I could to shut her so-called school down and to rescue the girls whose parents have dumped them there."

"It's not all bad," Rebecca said, wincing again as the carriage rocked into motion. "I don't know what I would do without Jo and Caro, and I met them there. I also learned French and German. Well, a bit."

"It's not worth it," Nigel grumbled. "Nothing can possibly make what was done to you right."

Part of Rebecca wanted to continue arguing in favor of her friends, since she never would have known them without the school. But she had almost no energy left. Her body ached, and all she wanted to do was snuggle against Nigel and forget the world.

"I'm certain Verity will be more than happy to harbor Lady Rebecca," Lord Landsbury said, "until such a time as—"

"No." Nigel cut him off. Rebecca shifted to glance questioningly up at him. "Tell your driver to take us to my flat by Hyde Park."

"Your flat?" Lord Landsbury repeated. Rebecca couldn't tell if he was studying her with disapproval or with shock. Either way, he knocked on the roof of the carriage, then leaned out the window to tell the driver, "Hamilton Place." As soon as he was seated once more, he arched a brow at Nigel and asked, "Are you sure you know what you're doing?"

"Yes," Nigel answered unequivocally. "I've never been more sure in my life."

Rebecca smiled and rested her head against Nigel's shoulder. Her position wasn't comfortable, but within moments she had drifted into a contented half-sleep. She awoke fully when the carriage came to a stop and sat straight. With a little effort, Nigel carried her out of the carriage without her feet having to touch the ground. Lord Landsbury stepped out with them.

"Are you planning on finishing your business in the pub?" he asked, nodding to The Silver Hart.

Nigel stared longingly at the pub for a moment before letting out a heavy breath and shaking his head. "There are more things in the world than catching thieves. I know where I'm needed now."

"Is that what you were in there for?" Lord Landsbury asked.

"Catching thieves?" Rebecca added.

Nigel looked from her to Lord Landsbury. "If that was the diamond thief earlier, then there's little chance he's still in the pub. All I know is that it couldn't be Herrington."

"That's the man you nearly knocked over on Manchester Square," Lord Landsbury said.

Nigel nodded. "Herrington is not the thief. But that doesn't rule out Lichfield, and I still believe the two are associated somehow."

"Then we need to find them," Rebecca said, making a half-hearted effort to wriggle out of Nigel's arms.

"No," he said, smiling at her. "They can wait for another day. Tonight, my only concern is you."

"Oh." Rebecca could feel her blush from her cheeks to the tips of her toes.

"Good luck, man," Lord Landsbury told Nigel with a wink.

He returned to his carriage and Nigel headed toward the door of his building. As far as Rebecca was concerned, he was extraordinarily agile in the way he carried her inside, up the stairs, and unlocked the door to his flat with her in his arms. Nothing had changed since the afternoon, but Rebecca felt as though she were coming home after a long journey. Nigel shut the door behind her and carried her straight to his bedroom.

She swallowed a sound of discomfort as he lowered her to the bed, instantly rolling to her side and letting out a breath of relief. "That's better."

"That woman is a devil," Nigel growled, reaching for her feet and tugging off her slippers. "I cannot be responsible for what I might do if I ever see her again." With her shoes removed, he slipped off her stockings.

"You'll have to see her when I go back," she said. A titillating thrill of pleasure began to pulse through her as he undressed her. When her stockings were gone, he shifted up to tug loose the ties of her gown.

"You aren't going back," he said with a note of ferocity. "You're staying right here, with me."

Rebecca twisted to glance over her shoulder at him even as he pushed the top of her bodice down over her shoulders. "Stay with you?" Her heart beat faster as she remembered what he'd told Miss Dobson in parting.

He seemed to sense her true question. "I'm going to marry you, Rebecca Burgess, make no mistake about that."

Rebecca sucked in a breath as a shiver passed through her. "My parents will never consent."

"Your parents aren't in England at present," Nigel reminded her. He gestured for her to rock back to her knees, and when she did, he proceeded to peel her gown up over her head and to toss it aside.

"If they find out I've married a Bow Street Runner, they might come back and attempt to have the marriage annulled," she said.

He shook his head, removing her stays and sweeping her chemise up over her head, leaving her fully naked. "If they do return, all they'll discover is that you've married the Baron Wharton."

Rebecca pursed her lips and frowned at him in confusion. "Nigel, I have no intention of marrying anyone but you."

He merely stared back at her, a slight twitch to his lips that might have been a smile, his eyes alive with mirth and desire.

A moment later, Rebecca caught on. Her mouth dropped open, but it took another moment before she had the sense to say, "You're Baron Wharton?"

"The tenth Baron Wharton, to be exact," he said, his

smile growing. "Or I will be when my father's time on this earth is over."

Rebecca scooted around so that she could look more fully at him. His revelation was such a surprise that she barely registered she was having the conversation stark naked. "But if you're a baron to be, why are you living in a tiny flat and working as a Bow Street Runner?" Although it suddenly made sense how he could afford a flat in such a prestigious location.

"My sister was violated," Nigel answered, suddenly serious. More than serious, he was furious. "I refused to stand by and do nothing. I worked with the Runners to find her attacker. As it happened, I had a talent for investigation. Gibbon—my superior—offered me a job. My father was so proud of what I'd done to protect Emmaline, that he gave his blessing."

"How unusual," Rebecca said. She started to sit, but was reminded of how sore her backside was and bounced up to her knees once more.

Nigel's face darkened again. "Catching diamond thieves is one thing, but I have no patience whatsoever for anyone who hurts women, even other women."

He moved closer to her and helped her to lay on her stomach once more. Rebecca expected pity or deeper anger from him, but when she turned her head to the side to gauge his expression, a sensual smolder lit his eyes. That look sent a whole new kind of heat to her nether region.

"I hate that she did this to you," he said in a rough voice, studying her backside.

She opened her mouth to reassure him that the worst of it was over now, but he reached out, caressing her tender backside. The sting of pain returned, but with it an almost incomprehensible rush of pleasure. That pleasure only increased as he stroked her punished flesh.

"If it hurts too much, tell me to stop," he said, his voice little more than a rumble.

"Don't stop," she sighed, tilting her hips up toward him.

But he did stop. Ripples of disappointment shot through her as his weight left the bed. At least until she realized he'd stood in order to shed his clothes.

Desire pulsed through her, and she pushed up to her knees once more as he yanked off his boots and threw them aside. She watched, enraptured, as he shrugged out of his jacket, unbuttoned his waistcoat, and pulled it and his shirt off over his head. He reached for the falls of his breeches, but Rebecca stopped him.

"Let me," she said. "Please let me."

Nigel studied her with passion-hooded eyes before moving to the side of the bed. His breeches were already tented, and she went to work enthusiastically undoing the buttons so that she could free him. Her sex squeezed in anticipation as his cock lifted free of its confinement. She sighed in satisfaction as she pushed his breeches down over his hips, then took him in both hands.

"I wanted to explore you this afternoon," she said breathlessly, "but you wouldn't let me."

"I wouldn't have lasted," he said, sucking in a breath and growling as she stroked his length.

He seemed to grow in her hands, becoming as hard as iron. "But now?"

"Now, I'll hold back for as long as you want."

A mischievous giggle tickled the back of her throat. That wasn't the only thing she wanted tickling the back of her throat, though. She tested the weight of his sack with one hand, feeling him tense at the touch, while rubbing her thumb around the flared head of his penis. Already, a touch of pearl was forming there.

Her sex throbbed with excitement as she bent forward to lick that dot. He sucked in a breath, which she found so irresistible that she licked him again. She did more than that. She kissed the tip of his penis, then again with her mouth open. His taste was masculine and salty, and instantly she wanted more.

She brought the whole head of his penis into her mouth, flickering her tongue across the underside. An uninhibited sigh of satisfaction ripped out of him. She wanted to hear more of that. She wanted him moaning uncontrollably, the way she had when he'd been so deep inside of her. So she drew him in deeper, relaxing her mouth and throat as much as she could. It was fascinating, scintillating, to pleasure him that way. She pulled back a bit, then drew him in deeper, over and over until she felt she could swallow him more fully.

"Darling, you're killing me," Nigel groaned at one point. But when she stopped to glance questioningly up at him, he said, "Keep on killing me."

She grinned, then took him into her mouth once more. Whenever she'd seen her sister Mary do the same to Lord Grey, she'd always felt a bit of revulsion. But, in fact, as she bore down on Nigel, challenging herself to see how much of him she could take, power surged through her. She had the power to make this huge, fierce man cry out with pleasure, to make him lose control. She even felt powerful when he grabbed fists full of her hair and guided her to move faster, taking him deeper.

Just when she felt something shift in him and the tension within his body mount, he stepped away, his cock slipping out of her mouth with an almost comical sound.

"Not this way," he panted. "In you."

Rebecca's sex throbbed in response. She was exhausted, sore, and her backside continued to sting, but all she wanted was to spread her legs and have him plunder her. She wanted to feel the heat of him bursting within her, knowing his seed could take hold.

He climbed onto the bed with her, but rather than splaying her on her back, he lifted her so that she was kneeling in front of him, facing away from him. Her burning backside nestled against the curve of his hips, but the sting was nothing to the pleasure pulsing through her. He reached around, closing his hands around her breasts and kneading them.

"So soft," he growled. He jerked his hips against hers.

The thick heat of his cock wedged between her legs, rubbing against her aching sex in a way that was deliciously teasing without satisfying. He continued to squeeze her breasts, working her nipples into hard points.

"Do you want me to fuck you?" he growled against her ear. She sighed with need. "After everything you've been through this evening? Do you want my hard cock deep in your pussy?"

"Yes," she sighed. She'd never meant the word more in her life.

At least, not until Nigel asked, "Do you want to be my wife? Do you want me to fuck you senseless every night? Do you want me to fill your womb with babies?" He pinched both of her nipples as he asked.

She gasped at the sensation, then groaned, "Yes, yes, dear God, yes." She was shocked at how frantic and needy her words sounded, but she wasn't at all surprised at how desperately she meant them.

"My Rebecca," Nigel purred against her ear. He slipped one hand from her breast to her sex, parting her folds so that he could stroke her clitoris. "My wife."

The sensations he ignited in her were so powerful that they eclipsed all of the pain and humiliation she'd experienced. Her body was already on fire, but it seemed to be engulfed in flame as his hand worked on her. She was so primed and ready that in no time at all she gasped and cried out as she came.

The throbbing pleasure had only begun when he bent her forward, spreading her knees and lifting her hips. She barely had time to balance on her forearms before he guided himself to her entrance and thrust home. She cried out as her already tender body protested for a moment, but that moment of soreness was eclipsed by the bone-deep pleasure of having him fill her. It was an entirely different sensation from what she'd experienced that afternoon, but amazing all the same. He stretched her, stroked her, and filled her to the point of breaking. She'd challenged herself to take him deeper and deeper into her mouth, and now he seemed to be doing the same with his cock sinking farther and farther into her quim with each thrust. She could feel him so deep within her that when he did finally tense and cry out in orgasm, she was certain his seed shot straight to her womb.

At last, he groaned and released her, and they both tumbled, thoroughly spent, to the bed. Rebecca's cheeks blazed with the afterglow of their mating. As hot as she was, it was bliss when Nigel pulled her into his arms, shielding her bruised body with his powerful one.

"You're mine," he sighed, stroking her sides and breasts as her back pressed into his chest. "Let someone else catch the diamond thief. I've caught you, and that's all that matters. You'll always be mine. I'll never let you feel hurt or slighted again. I'll only make you feel loved. I love you."

A pleasure far deeper than lust poured through every part of her. She felt his promise as if it were the air she breathed and the sunlight that warmed her. "I love you too, Nigel," she said in return, reaching back to rest a hand on his hip. "And I promise I'll always make sure you feel it. I'll make you the happiest man alive."

"I'm already the happiest man alive," Nigel said, closing a hand around her breast and pinching her nipple. "I have you."

EPILOGUE

*J*o's heart was filled with joy as she and Caro stood on the stairs of Miss Dobson's school, watching Mr. Kent carry Rebecca out of the wretched place and off to what Jo could only hope would be a magnificent new life. She'd seen everything that Miss Dobson had done to poor Rebecca in the wine cellar, and she didn't think she would ever be able to forgive the wicked old woman, especially as she knew everything Miss Dobson said was pure hypocrisy.

"This is outrageous," Miss Dobson railed once Mr. Kent and Rebecca and Lord Landsbury were gone. She whipped to face the throng of young ladies who had clustered in the hallway to watch the unfolding drama. "Let this be a lesson to you all," she went on, her head held high and her nose in the air. "Wicked little harlots get what is coming to them. Lady Rebecca will be ruined by this, utterly ruined. She'll never be able to hold her head up in polite society again. Is that what the lot of you want?"

The stunned girls watched her for a moment before Miss Conyer said, "No, miss," in a demanding voice.

"We would rather die," Miss Cade agreed, glaring at the pupils nearest her. "Wouldn't we?"

The others seemed to sense the tide had turned and if they wanted to keep their backsides pristine and their knuckles un-rapped, the best thing to do was to keep quiet and go along. One by one, they rushed back to whatever they had been doing before the scene had unfolded. Several charged up the stairs, likely heading for their bedrooms.

"We'd better retire for the evening," Caro whispered to Jo, glancing warily at Miss Dobson.

Jo nodded in agreement, but they were too late.

"You," Miss Dobson shouted, rushing halfway up the stairs. The other pupils scattered, probably fearing they'd be caught in whatever horrible net Miss Dobson was about to throw. "It was you, wasn't it?" She glared at Jo.

"Me, Miss Dobson?" Jo feigned innocence.

"You defended the wicked Lady Rebecca." Miss Dobson narrowed her eyes more as she came to a stop one step above Jo and Caro, likely so that she could tower over them. "You brought that man here."

"How could I have, miss?" Jo squeaked, pretending to be far more afraid of Miss Dobson than she was.

"You and Lady Caroline are thick as thieves with

Lady Rebecca. You were the ones who sounded the alarm," Miss Dobson went on.

"We couldn't have, miss," Caro said, pretending to cower right along with Jo. "Other than the fact that we wouldn't dare, you know as well as anyone that we've been secure in the school all day."

"Yes," Jo said. "Miss Warren was guarding the door all day. And we were engaged in quiet contemplation in our room all afternoon."

"Miss Cade can attest to that," Caro added.

Miss Dobson bared her teeth in a snarl. She raised her hand slightly, and Jo was certain she was going to strike. But in the end, she lowered her arm and hissed a curse so salty it had Jo and Caro's eyebrows shooting up to their hairlines. "You're right," she hissed. "It couldn't have been you. But I'll find out who it was." She started back down the stairs, but just when Jo thought it was safe to continue up to their room, Miss Dobson snapped back to her, glaring. "I've got my eye on you. On both of you." She pointed a finger at Jo and Caro. "You're as degenerate as Lady Rebecca. I have no doubt that you'll show your true colors before long. I'll be ready."

With a final, sinister sneer, Miss Dobson turned and marched back down the stairs. Jo didn't breathe in relief until she and Caro had reached the next floor, and she didn't dare say a word until they were safe in their room.

"She doesn't know about the secret passageway," Jo said, flopping on her bed. "If she did, she would have realized how I got out."

"And you made it to Lord Landsbury's house without incident?" Caro asked. Instead of sitting, she paced the center of the room. "I'm so sorry that I was waylaid and couldn't continue on with you."

"It was a good thing you were stopped," Jo said, sitting straight. "Because now we know that Lord Herrington isn't the diamond thief."

"We don't know for certain," Caro said, rubbing her arms as she paced. "Although I was never convinced it was him in the first place."

"But the way you spoke to him," Jo went on. "The hints you dropped about wanting to purchase the diamond, of being willing to give him anything he wanted for it. He didn't know what you were talking about."

Caro flushed, a slow smile spreading across her lips. "He seemed interested enough in my offer to give him anything he asked for."

Jo blinked in surprise. Was that the sort of thing that had gone on between Caro and Lord Herrington after she'd rushed on to Lord Lansbury's house.

Caro shook her head and stopped pacing. "No, if what I've been told is correct, Lord Herrington is so desperate for money that he would have at least shown some interest in my offer. The poor thing knew he couldn't afford my other offer as well."

"Your other offer?"

Caro sent her a blunt look. "Gentlemen don't bed women if they know they can't afford the consequences. And I believe Lord Herrington is a good man."

"How do you know that?" Jo asked.

"Feminine intuition."

Jo eyed her skeptically. "He is rather handsome."

For a moment, she thought Caro would be upset. But then she giggled. A moment after that, she shook her head and resumed her pacing. "No, Lord Herrington isn't the diamond thief."

"So it must be Lord Lichfield," Jo reasoned.

"It could be any number of men," Caro sighed, sitting on her bed at last. "We have so much work to do."

"And I'm glad for it," Jo said, confidence welling within her. "It will give us something to think about besides how horrible this place is."

"It is horrible," Caro agreed. "I can't believe that Miss Dobson will be able to hold onto the place very long after today, though."

"But she owns it," Jo said. "There's no way to take it from her. The only way it would close is if too many parents withdrew their daughters. But I know my mother would never do that. Not after—" She pinched her mouth closed, embarrassment over the event that had branded her as bad and in need of reform in her parent's eyes rushing back in on her. She let out a breath and shook her head. "Let's focus on the diamond thief. Specifically, let's focus on Lord Lichfield.

"You believe he is the thief?" Caro asked.

"Yes, I do," Jo said. "And with a little luck, I'll be able to prove it."

§

I HOPE YOU'VE ENJOYED REBECCA AND NIGEL'S story! The two of them just had to end up together. But as you can see, the bigger story isn't over yet. Can Lord Rufus Herrington truly be ruled out as the diamond thief? Is Lord Felix Lichfield the real culprit? Or perhaps Mr. Wallace Newman? Or could it be Mr. Khan himself? Jo and Caro will keep on investigating, aided by the secret passageway.

But what happens when Jo's parents suddenly pull her out of school with the intent of marrying her off to a man desperate for a wife and an heir? What happens when that man turns out to be none other than Felix Lichfield himself? Can Jo prove he's the diamond thief or will her efforts to entrap him earn her a sexy spanking? Jo is about to find out just how Felix earned his sensual reputation...but the answer might not be what she or you think. Find out in Book 5 of *When the Wallflowers were Wicked, The Cheeky Minx.*

IF YOU ENJOYED THIS BOOK AND WOULD LIKE TO HEAR more from me, please sign up for my newsletter! When you sign up, you'll get a free, full-length novella, *A Passionate Deception.* Victorian identity theft has never been so exciting in this story of hope, tricks, and starting over. Part of my *West Meets East* series, *A Passionate Deception* can be read as a stand-alone. Pick up your free copy today by signing up to receive my newsletter (which I only send out when I have a new release)!

Sign up here: http://eepurl.com/cbaVMH

Click here for a complete list of other works by Merry Farmer.

ABOUT THE AUTHOR

I hope you have enjoyed *The Blushing Harlot*. If you'd like to be the first to learn about when new books in the series come out and more, please sign up for my newsletter here: http://eepurl.com/cbaVMH And remember, Read it, Review it, Share it! For a complete list of works by Merry Farmer with links, please visit http://wp.me/P5ttjb-14F.

Merry Farmer is an award-winning novelist who lives in suburban Philadelphia with her cats, Torpedo, her grumpy old man, and Justine, her hyperactive new baby. She has been writing since she was ten years old and realized one day that she didn't have to wait for the teacher to assign a creative writing project to write something. It was the best day of her life. She then went on to earn not one but two degrees in History so that she would always have something to write about. Her books have reached the Top 100 at Amazon, iBooks, and Barnes & Noble, and have been named finalists in the prestigious RONE and Rom Com Reader's Crown awards.

ACKNOWLEDGMENTS

I owe a huge debt of gratitude to my awesome beta-readers, Caroline Lee and Jolene Stewart, for their suggestions and advice. And double thanks to Julie Tague, for being a truly excellent editor and assistant! Thanks also to the members of the Historical Harlots Facebook Group, who provide me with all sorts of inspiration!

Click here for a complete list of other works by Merry Farmer.

Printed in Great Britain
by Amazon

50842902R00090